I0831530

THE NINE ORDERS

THE MATRICULATION

Q. J. ZEPHYR

This is a work of fiction. Names, characters, places, and incidents are either the product of the author's imagination or are used fictitiously. Any resemblance to actual persons, living or dead, events, or locales is entirely coincidental.

Book Design by MDW LTD Publishing

ISBN: (979-8-99019472-4)

Published by MDW LTD Publishing, LLC

www.the9orders.com

This book is dedicated to the matriarchs of my family, Lola Dorothy Swan. Your endless love, prodigious Jones, and faith, and unwavering support never faltered. The endurance that is required to write with the limited ability that I have was learned while watching you shoulder our dreams through stormy seas, always at the helm with happy hearts, capable hands, and a fair share of wit.

Contents

*Note to the reader: This book contains the introduction of a new character whose story begins just before The Collection. His narrative is interwoven with the current timeline already established by the author. Please do not let this confuse you as you read along. There are clues within the chapters dedicated to this character that will help you identify the appropriate temporal context. Thank you.

CHAPTER ONE
Happy Birthday

Brandon Tsang was the descendant of a storied legacy. His ancestors once ruled China as it transitioned away from Mongol rule. Brandon's grandfather had been a member of the sacred *Yi he Quan*, commonly referred to as the 'Boxers' of the infamous rebellion which fought valiantly against the forces of Western imperialism. Since that time, the Tsang family stopped at nothing to reinsert Chinese interests into the global marketplace. Their die-hard ambitions wore away at the traditional values that once rooted the ancient clan. Many aspects of their cultural heritage had been stripped away by the cumulative effects of hardline communism and rapid modernization. Yet, with great sacrifice, a horde of material wealth took their place. Brandon, an heir to an heir, never had to endure the rice famines during the Qing Dynasty or the shame his grandfather suffered after being exiled to Taiwan. The young man was born into an age of digital connectivity, covert economic policies, and borderless warfare.

Brandon had attended primary and secondary school in Finland where he chose to live with his brutal and exacting grandfather. Tsang Xi Huan was an ex-Kuomintang commander, who instilled in Brandon a deep respect for authority. Xi Huan was also a master of a fighting style that had been passed down to generations of Tsang men called Bao Quan or 'wrapped fist'.

Brandon's grandfather beat the tenets of Bao Quan into his grandson. As a result, the young boy learned how to both take a punch and think on his feet. Brandon flourished in the ultra-strict environment and gained early admittance into Cambridge where he graduated with a degree in international commerce at the age of twenty. He went on to study at Harvard Business School where he earned an MBA. It was then that his grandfather passed away. But while Tsang Xi Huan lay on his deathbed, he gripped his grandson's hand like a vice, and, without a word of praise, slapped the sacred brass ring of Bao Quan into his palm. The gesture symbolized the passing down of secret knowledge which forever connected the young man to his forebears. The power of the ring's possession gave Brandon the confidence he needed to forge headfirst into a complex world he knew little about.

The Tsang estate rested on a fortune built from the darkest corners of human existence. It was said that death, itself, owed the Tsang clan taxes as it drifted through the rotting underbelly of the waking world. Brandon's father, Charlie, had done his best to legitimize the Tsang financial empire by founding China's first private bank. The Tsang Tao Bank grew exponentially by employing a different economic model than the rest of its subsidized competitors. Consequently, the bank fattened itself as it monopolized a considerable portion of the Southeast Asian economic corridor.

Charlie Tsang refused to learn Bao Quan. The progressive banker thought it a relic of a bygone era. This was a constant source of enmity between Charlie and Xi Huan while the old man was still living. Their mutual contempt for one another knew no bounds and often left Brandon struggling for an acceptance that neither man was willing to give. Despite that, Charlie had become his own man by vastly increasing the family's assets. But Charlie, unbeknownst to anyone in his family, had sold his soul to a small band of extraordinarily powerful people known only as the Order. The establishment of the Tsang Tao Bank was solely to procure membership in the deadly cabal. The Order required unconditional access to their members' finances for reasons of its own, no questions asked. In return, its members became gods among men. Their personal and economic whims melted through jurisdictional hindrances like lasers. In a world of such high rewards, the risks to others who dealt with the Order were beyond mere death. The Order had the ability to influence the fortunes of people for generations to come.

Charlie Tsang had only recently come to appreciate the scope of the Order's ambitions when he was warned about their plot to usher in a new world order. In exchange for the protection of his immediate family, Charlie had been ordered to deliver his firstborn son into the hands of the shadowy organization. Charlie knew his wife would mourn the loss of their only son, whom she all but worshipped. He also knew that when the Order called upon one of its own for any reason, you did what they asked without hesitation.

Charlie had gained a notable reputation within the Order for executing their demands more expediently than his western counterparts. He had every intention of offering up his son with the same unshakable resolve. Just before the onset of the collection, Charlie prepared an extravagant dinner in the most luxurious hotel in Hong Kong to celebrate his son's twenty-fifth birthday. Charlie thought it an excellent opportunity for Brandon, who had just completed a highly coveted internship at Deutsche Bank, to see his family one last time.

“Mother, please tell me what this is all about,” Brandon asked while looking over the hundreds of well-dressed guests in the stately ballroom of the Royal Meridian.

“What? Your father isn’t allowed to be proud of his son’s accomplishments?” Vivian Tsang answered after taking a sip from a tall glass of champagne. She turned toward Brandon and rested her shrewd eyes on him.

“You and I both know this party has nothing to do with my accomplishments.”

“Don’t be silly. You have just graduated from the finest university in the world. Besides, it is good for our shareholders to meet their next chairman in person. I am sure you will make a good impression.”

“I don’t recall work ever being a part of most people’s birthday celebrations.”

“You are not most people, my son. You are a Tsang. Now stop fussing and introduce yourself to that man over there in the ugly brown suit. His name is Mr. Liu…”

“Liu Zhuang Yi, head of the largest telecommunications company in China. I know who he is.”

“Good. Then you should know that he is your father’s biggest investor. He also happens to have a beautiful daughter who is not yet married. She is finishing her last year at Berkeley and will soon return to Hong Kong to help manage his company."

"Always the matchmaker. You're far better at playing these games of false interest than I am. Are you sure you don't want to become chairman instead?" he groaned as he watched Liu's greasy, bulbous fingers picking at the shrimp buffet.

"I have no desire to rule over our estate, my son. I have only the desire to serve, which requires far more tact. Now, get over there and introduce yourself."

"Okay, I will tell him that you are attracted to him. What room shall I say you're staying in since it is definitely not with father?"

His mother's eyes widened. She balked at her son's brazen disregard for filial piety. She then remembered they shared the same morbid sense of humor especially when feeling anxious.

"One of these days your tongue will get you into trouble. Maybe if you were married it would be too tired to speak such nonsense."

"Or maybe it would become that much stronger," Brandon countered. That's how it was between the two of them, always a battle of wits to a stalemate. Their love for one another kept their gloves on even though they routinely hit below the belt. "Mother, I'm going. There's no need to give me snake eyes."

"It is not the snake's eyes you should be concerned with. It's her bite," she replied, holding two of her fingers up to her mouth to resemble a pair of fangs. "Now go."

Brandon introduced himself to Mr. Liu, who was grateful for the opportunity to finally meet Charlie's son, whom he'd heard so much about. They shared several casual jokes before moving on to discuss Liu's business prospects. Mr. Liu was in the beginning phases of developing a line of cell phones set for national distribution. He wanted Brandon's input on whether Myanmar or Senegal would be the ideal location for his manufacturing facilities. Brandon was extolling the virtues of China's own technological infrastructure when he was interrupted by his father, who didn't join the conversation as much as steamroll right over it.

"Ah, I see you have met Liu Zhuang Yi!" Charlie smiled grabbing a hold of his son's shoulder. Brandon skillfully slipped from under his father's false display of affection. "You know, Brandon, Mr. Liu's daughter is very beautiful, and I hear she is coming back to China. Is this true, my friend?"

"Yes, thank you. Sarah is, indeed, a very beautiful young woman, and she has expressed to me her desire to marry a Chinese man," Mr. Liu added, proud of his family's penchant for tradition.

"We must introduce the two of them soon," Charlie suggested, stooping over Liu while pointing to his son.

"Yes, she will return in a few months. We will let our wives arrange it."

"Excellent." Charlie shook Mr. Lui's hand. "You must excuse us. There are some very powerful men I wish to introduce my son to."

"Yes, uh…very well." Mr. Liu stammered at the slight disrespect shown to him. Charlie Tsang was known for talking down to people below his station but never with contempt or hatred, just an honest and open disregard for their feelings.

"It was nice meeting you, Mr. Liu. I look forward to being introduced to Sarah. I'm sure she is lovely." Brandon shook Mr. Liu's hand and followed his father to the private elevator used only by the most select patrons of the hotel.

"Where are we going?" Brandon asked as the sounds of clinking champagne glasses and soft jazz faded away into the background. He was annoyed by the lack of manners Charlie had shown Liu and didn't understand why his father was even speaking with him. The man usually avoided his son like the plague when around such lofty company.

"As I said, there is a very important man that I must introduce you to. He is here, in Hong Kong, on business and would very much like to wish you a happy birthday in person."

"Why doesn't he just come to the party?"

"This man is extremely private. I'm quite sure he wouldn't want to be seen in my company."

Brandon couldn't tell if his father was drunk, high, or both. He shrugged off Charlie's quizzical behavior and stepped inside the elevator with him. Charlie pushed the button for the uppermost penthouse.

While *en route* Charlie turned to his son and sighed heavily. "Brandon, are you prepared to do whatever it takes to move our family forward?"

"Why do you even have to ask?" Brandon answered, irritated at the insinuation that he had decided to help run his father's enterprises without thinking it through. "If I didn't want to be here, I would've taken the job at Deutsche Bank."

"Every man must make his own way in this world. I am wondering if you are ready to do what must be done to ensure the survival of our great legacy." Charlie peered into his son's eyes searching for an unknown qualia. "I know I have shown you the back of my hand ever since you deserted your mother and me by moving in with your grandfather. But now, all that is in the past. Here, you stand before me no longer a boy, but a man. And as a man, it is important to put other's needs ahead of your own."

"The back of your hand? You have never taken an interest in me father. You never attended any of my graduations, not one. Why are you telling me all this anyway?" Brandon was getting angry over his father's usual callousness, but the awkwardness of the situation was cut short by the beep that signaled the elevator's arrival on the top floor. Charlie didn't answer his son and walked out of the elevator toward the black double doors of the presidential suite. He knocked on the door three times in rapid succession. They were opened from the inside by a man wearing a shoulder holster with what amounted to a hand cannon stuck inside it. Brandon and Charlie were welcomed into the lavishly appointed suite. Sitting cross-legged by himself, yet surrounded by a small contingent of dangerous-looking men carrying automatic rifles, sat an unassuming gentleman wearing a tuxedo and smoking a cigar. The man in the tux seemed pleased to see them but didn't stand upon their arrival as social convention dictated. Instead, he invited his guests to sit opposite him on a black leather sofa of impeccable modernist design.

"Ah, the two heads of the mighty dragon! Welcome. It is an honor to finally meet you, Brandon. I wish you an incredibly transcendent twenty-fifth birthday." the short balding man said in a thick Belgian accent. He leaned forward to shake Brandon's hand from a seated position which the young man thought was strange. The man didn't immediately let go. Instead, he squeezed tightly goading Brandon to shake hands more firmly. Brandon obliged but stopped after noticing the Belgian wince. A small inconspicuous drop of blood fell unseen from underneath Brandon's cuff. "My goodness, young man, that is quite the handshake. My name is Gregori Olivier. Your father and I are very close business associates. Whenever I find myself in Hong Kong I like to meet with him if our schedules allow it. He tells me you were at the top of your class at Harvard. That is certainly a notable achievement. You should be very proud."

"Thank you very much, Mr. Olivier. But I must say, your name doesn't ring a bell. What industry are you in?" Brandon asked as a matter of small talk and base curiosity. Brandon had a knack for knowing who worked where. It was all part and parcel of being a top-performing portfolio manager. His ears perked as he waited for Olivier's response.

"I collect rare antiquities from East Asia and the Levant. Your father and I often bid against each other at auction which is how I came to be his acquaintance. I have, unfortunately, lost out to his egregious spending habits on many an occasion." Olivier answered while looking at Charlie who simply nodded his head in agreement. Brandon eyed his father with suspicion. He might as well have been kowtowing to Olivier. Charlie never played second fiddle to anyone, even when he was around high-level Chinese officials. Brandon knew he was in the presence of someone of great importance though he didn't quite understand the nature of the power dynamic at play.

"I never knew dealing in antiquities could be such a dangerous business," Brandon joked, looking around at Olivier's security detail.

"Yes, well, when traveling as much as I do, especially to the places I frequent, one learns very quickly that you can never be too careful," Olivier said, ashing his cigar into a gilded dragon-shaped ashtray resting on the glass coffee table that sat between them. "Can I offer you a celebratory glass of whiskey? Japan's finest."

"Of course," Brandon accepted. Olivier had one of his armed guards bring over a fifteen year-old bottle of Yamazaki along with three tumblers, each with a solid round ice cube the size of a golf ball inside.

“I admire your taste in whiskey,” Brandon complimented the Belgian while sampling the smoky single malt.

“Cheers! To health, wealth, and happiness!” Olivier smiled clinking glasses with his guests. The Belgian relished the taste of the sweet brown liquor, then set his tumbler on an end table to his right. He fixed his gaze on Brandon trying to hide his jealousy of the young man’s good looks. “Brandon, the reason I have asked your father to bring you here is that I would like to give you a wonderful, yet, rather impromptu birthday present.”

“Really? I am honored.” Brandon’s face brightened. The birthday boy assumed the present would be a luxurious watch or something of the sort.

“It will, however, require a bit of travel. I promise that if you do decide to accept my gift you will be exposed to a world very few people have ever had the privilege of experiencing. I’m afraid I cannot divulge more for fear it would ruin the surprise.”

“Travel?” Brandon asked, studying his father’s passive smile. “I don’t know. I mean, it would be rude of me to leave my own birthday party without saying goodbye to everyone.”

“Yes, I understand all that, but your father has assured me that your worry is unnecessary. I have a plane waiting for you on the roof just up those stairs," Olivier replied, gesturing toward a darkened stairwell tucked in the corner of the suite.

"A plane? How in the world did you manage to land a plane on the roof?" Brandon asked with a look of astonishment.

"It's called vertical take-off. It's rather pedestrian by now. Surely you've heard of it."

"Of course, but only military planes are licensed to use it," Brandon countered, knowing the law well. His good friend and fellow Harvard alum, Gabriel Artista, owned and operated a private commuter airline. He had flown with Gabriel countless times and had learned a lot about modern aviation in the process.

"Yes, well, let's just say everyone turns a blind eye to the fact that I own one," Olivier replied through thick curling wisps of cigar smoke.

"Brandon, just go. You'll be back here in a matter of hours. I will send a car for you when you return. Look, I know I haven't always done right by you. But consider this present an opportunity for me to show how grateful I am to call you my son," Charlie said as he put his hand on Brandon's shoulder. The instant he did Brandon began to feel light-headed. The young man looked over at Olivier, whose face warbled in the light.

“Okay, sure.” Brandon slobbered as his face went numb. A few seconds later the twenty-five year-old slumped down on the sofa where he sat and gently nodded off. Charlie just sat there grinning at his unconscious prodigy. He lifted his hands toward Olivier as if to present an offering, “He is yours to do as the Order pleases.”

“Very well. You may take your leave, Mr. Tsang. Take comfort in the knowledge that the roots and the branches of your family tree shall grow unfettered in every direction,” Olivier said in a voice as cold and sharp as glass. Charlie stood up and tugged at the hem of his tuxedo jacket. He regarded his son’s peaceful face with a look of finality and then returned to the party alone.

As soon as Charlie left, Olivier’s guards sprang into action. They carried Brandon’s body to the roof of the hotel where a large black carbon fiber drone, fitted with a compartment large enough to house a human body, awaited. Brandon was placed inside and strapped down. One of the guards implanted a glowing RFID chip in Brandon’s right hand and then secured the drone compartment’s lid. The armed men left the roof as the drone ascended into the night sky and disappeared beyond the rainbow-colored lights of Victoria Harbor.

CHAPTER TWO

Ruby

Leila headed east past the border of South Africa in a zombie-like daze. The memory of her mother and father weighed heavily upon her. Each step she took away from the shelters felt like a betrayal. Days turned into weeks and the voice that had spoken to her from within her dream hadn't so much as whispered. The confidence that had bubbled up inside her was gone and was replaced with the very real notion that she was alone, again.

The reptilian guard had told her the truth about the storms. There were no signs of them or their foretold damage. Everything was just as it had been except for the unforgiving heat and humidity. Leila clung to the shadows of vacant buildings moving about mostly at night like a church mouse in hopes of avoiding unwanted hazards. Now and then Leila would spy on small bands of foragers searching for anything they could salvage. She felt little sympathy for them and never once thought of sharing the food in her pack with any of them. She considered surface dwellers to be lucky. They were free to breathe the open air and feel the warm summer winds against their skin which was far better than the balmy stench of the shelters. Leila couldn't understand why the government had lied about the storms. It didn't make any sense. She gave up trying to comprehend what was happening and simply kept walking, her head low.

Leila quietly hid herself away in the back of a trailer attached to an RV that belonged to an older couple. After a few days of traveling through Krueger National Park Leila hopped out and made her way to the wistful coastline of Mozambique. She could tell where she was because the language of the street signs had changed from Afrikaans to Portuguese. The dry terrain of the midlands had given way to beautiful beaches whose white sands sparkled in the midday sun. Leila looked upon the inviting landscape with new eyes. The crystalline waters no longer reminded her of the glints of light in her father's eyes. The sea had become an esoteric world filled with life, death, and a universe of unknowns. Leila threw her backpack onto the sand and dove into the clear blue sea. She surrendered herself as though she were being baptized by Mother Nature. When she rose from the Pacific Ocean a new person emerged. She was no longer "the girl from the shelters who had lost her parents". She was stronger. Leila wanted to live, not in fear, but with a joyful, open heart. She now understood that she was but an infinitesimally small part of a larger, more complex world. And so Leila explored the local marine life amidst the shoals that surrounded her and did her best to remain hopeful that she would one day be reunited with her mother and father.

One morning, after returning from a swim to a nearby sandbar, Leila sunned herself on a limestone outcropping that overlooked the beach. As she observed the multi-colored hexagons reflected by the sun against her wet eyelashes, she sensed a small movement to her side. She wasn't startled and didn't react right away to the tiny fluttering sounds she heard. Instead, she made a game of guessing what kind of animal was making the noise. When she finally turned her head she was pleased that her prediction had been correct. There, on the ledge beside her, partially hidden by a dried-out bulb of seaweed, lay a tiny grass snake writhing in the sun. The snake was as red as a jewel with tiny purple and yellow accents on its sides. Upon closer inspection, Leila saw that it had three puncture wounds in the middle of its body. Her compassion for the animal was immediate. Yet when she reached out for the snake the most peculiar thing happened. As soon as her fingertips touched the snake's warm scales a stream of images raced through her mind. She saw that the snake had been gripped by the sharp talons of a sea hawk. The hawk, after seizing the snake, had flown too close to a colony of terns who joined forces to repel the intruder from their midst. Amid the melee that ensued, the hawk dropped the snake on the rocks below leaving it to die alone. Leila cradled the small reptile in her lap and named it Ruby after its rich coloration. Sacrificing one of her water bottles, Leila bathed Ruby. The water cooled the snake's body which seemed to affect the tiny creature in a good way. She then tried her best to clean the snake's wounds without hurting it. A wide smile spread across Leila's face. She had found a measure of happiness in taking care of the snake, who seemed trapped somewhere between life and death.

Leila resolved to nurse Ruby back to health. As she hunted for food to feed the snake a newfound sense of purpose flowed from her spirit. Her instincts told her to find bugs that were large enough to provide a good meal but small enough to fit into the snake's little mouth. After an hour of searching, Leila came upon a dead cricket being eaten, bit by bit, by a small contingent of ants. She picked it up in her hands and blew it clean with her breath. It was the first time she had ever handled an insect on purpose without squealing like a pig. She took the dead insect to a shaded spot underneath a squat rubber tree. There she sat, Ruby in her lap, waiting for the snake to eat. But Ruby was uninterested in the dead cricket. After flicking the insect's body with its tongue several times, Ruby simply coiled up and rested. Leila thought that maybe Ruby wanted to die. It suddenly occurred to her that maybe the snake wanted to eat live crickets. After all, if a human was hungry you wouldn't just plop a live chicken in front of them and, maybe for animals, it was the reverse. So, with the snake wrapped around her forearm, Leila tried her hand at catching live crickets. It didn't take her long to trap several of them inside an empty plastic bottle. Leila emptied everything from her backpack and placed one of the crickets inside her pack along with the snake. She then waited patiently to see if her instincts had been correct.

Several minutes passed and the bag still lay motionless. Leila trained her ear for any noises coming from inside the pack. Finally, one of the corners of the bag bulged, and then, silence. Leila knew the deed had been done and zealously unzipped the pack. She was thrilled to see that Ruby had eaten the bug. Before letting the snake out she put two more crickets inside and zipped the pack closed again. She wanted to give Ruby a chance to fill up. The snake's appetite lived up to the moment and twenty minutes later when Leila reopened the bag none of the crickets could be found. She smiled and kissed the snake which in return crapped white fluid all over her arm. Leila rejoiced and dashed into the sea to clean herself off with Ruby in her hand. She could tell that Ruby didn't like seawater. It slithered up her shoulder eventually wrapping itself around the young girl's neck to avoid being splashed. Leila felt a lasting bond forming with Ruby and her wayward steps toward nowhere in particular became meaningful quests for crickets, beetles, and grasshoppers.

Leila's water supply had dwindled to half a bottle. It was time for her to leave the coastline in search of fresh water. She didn't want to leave the beaches but understood that it was necessary. North of her, along the beachhead, a small delta delivered silt from further inland. Leila decided to track the small rivulet back into the hills from which it came. Maybe it would lead her to more water. So, she and Ruby began to follow the waterway up into the foothills of Mozambique.

The terrain became dry and flat once again. Leila looked forward to reaching the hills for there was little shade in the lowlands. There was, however, plenty of food for Ruby and the snake seemed to be on a healthy road to recovery. One afternoon, Leila woke up from napping underneath a tall shrub to find that her tiny friend had shed its skin. She picked up the cast skin and held it up against the sun. The holes where the sea hawk's talons had left their mark could clearly be seen. Leila searched for any sign of the wounds in the snake's new skin but found nothing. She marveled at Ruby's ability to recover from such a traumatic event. She began to think of herself as a snake. She too had undergone a similar transformation. Leila wondered if the snake's personality had changed as well, but found little evidence in Ruby's behavior to suggest that it had. Maybe Leila hadn't changed all that much either. There was no way to tell for sure. Only her mother and father could help her answer that question. Leila doubled over in pain at the thought of her parents. Grief and loss tugged at her insides pulling her closer and closer into an inner realm of dread. She sobbed quietly heaving up sorrow like a shovel digging a grave. After her tears ran dry and the rush of remembrance was spent, Leila moved on driven by the overriding power of thirst.

The small river widened at the base of the foothills. It meandered down from its source and split into a network of streams before rejoining itself now and again. The narrow streams appeared too dirty to drink so Leila started to climb while listening out for the splashing of a waterfall or some other indication of fresh water. Soon the hike became arduous and the ten year-old found herself having to use the roots of trees and shrubs to hoist herself up through the steep brush. She eventually looked back down, unsure of her path, and saw that she had traveled quite a distance. It was pointless going back down, she thought. It would take even more energy to retrace her path than it would to simply continue onward. The panoramic view from her mid-mountain perch was motivation enough to go even higher. The flatlands below were vast and only the sea, not the beaches, could be seen. Leila turned back around to resume her ascent but surprisingly came face to face with a small curious baboon. Leila froze not knowing what to do. She tried not to look directly into the monkey's eyes but it was no use. Her smell, demeanor, and the red snake coiled around her arm were reason enough for the young baboon to shriek in fear for its own life. Having lived in South Africa for most of her childhood, Leila knew the danger baboons posed to human beings. They had little to no fear of people and routinely trespassed into homes and offices alike in search of food. The baboon bolted, disappearing over a ledge some twenty meters above.

Leila wasted no time. She knew baboons loved to bask in the sun. So she cut an angle to the dark side of the mountain in hopes of avoiding them altogether. It wasn't long before she heard the gruff grunts and stiff cackling of adult baboons. The violent sounds drove Leila to move even faster but the farther she traveled the closer the sounds became. She looked above her and saw that an entire clan of baboons was shadowing her path. They had begun to throw loose objects at the little girl. Leila was in a panic. Dodging missile after missile, she desperately grabbed hold of a vine and leaped into the air. The young girl covered a tremendous amount of ground as she swung out and away from her pursuers. Unfortunately, the vine she had chosen was water-deprived and snapped at its base. Leila and Ruby went tumbling down, end over end halted only by a rotted-out tree trunk. Leila picked herself up and ran down the mountain as fast as her spindly legs could carry her. The shrill hooting of baboons filled her ears. She dared not look back for fear of what she might find. Up ahead, several hundred meters away, Leila spied the white roof of an SUV with a great deal of luggage strapped to its top. She cried out for help hoping some brave camper might come to her aid. The baboons' screeches were so close she was sure they were going to overtake her. After deftly jumping over a large boulder and landing successfully, Leila's foot was swiped from behind her. The young girl rolled downhill like a pinball glancing off anything and everything her small body came into contact with. Regrettably, Ruby flew off Leila's forearm and disappeared into a thick bed of dry brush. Leila quickly recovered but found herself surrounded by a pack of heavy-breathing mandrills. Leila's heart sank as she observed their menacing ribbed faces. It was as though they wore blue and red masks of death. One mandrill tugged at Leila's backpack forcefully from behind. Leila swatted at it with a branch she had picked up from the ground. Before she could get to her feet, the king of the mandrill clan approached her, cautiously. Its short scruffy tail was curled upward and away from its buttocks in an obvious display of aggression. It roared at her, exposing its dagger-like incisors. Leila couldn't believe the size of its teeth. Where were they when its mouth was closed, she wondered? She removed her pack and threw it toward the imposing mandrill who batted it away with a powerful jut of its arm. Leila screamed at the top of her lungs. She was sure that this was the moment of her death. She backed away on all fours just as the terrifying mandrill lunged at her. The monkey grabbed her right foot and wrenched it back toward him dislocating it from her ankle. The pain was excruciating. Leila couldn't believe how strong the baboon was. She didn't want to see the rest. She closed her eyes and was about to resign herself to her fate when, suddenly, three ear-shattering gunshots rang out into the air from behind her. Leila opened her eyes and the mandrill that had been just inches from her face had run off to rejoin its troop. The baboons withdrew into the wilds of the mountain with her backpack in hand. Leila looked at her foot and threw up the little food she had remaining in her stomach when she saw it dangling to the side. A pair of strong arms picked her up from behind. Soft, consoling words blanketed the young girl who passed out shortly after from a combination of dehydration, heat exhaustion, and stress.

When Leila came to, she was riding in the back of the same SUV she had seen while trying to outrun the mandrills. It was a bumpy ride and the driver who had long, curly blonde hair was driving extremely fast.

"Xavier, she's awake. Slow down, mate. She's surely in a lot of pain," a man from the passenger side said with a lovely British accent. He looked Mediterranean and had gentle, olive-colored eyes.

"Where are you taking me?" Leila muffled, lifting her arm against her brow to block the view of her foot.

"We're taking you to a hospital. What were you doing out in the wilderness all by yourself? I mean, you must only be eleven or twelve?" the driver asked from the front seat.

"Where's Ruby?!" Leila cried. Her heart longed for the company of her colorful friend. "She's not here. Where is she?"

"What? There's another little girl back there?" The driver, upon hearing Leila's mention of another person, slammed on the brakes and waited for her response.

"No. Ruby's a snake. Where is she? I lost her!"

The man with the British accent sighed in relief and the driver accelerated again. "I'm sorry little one. She's gone, but I'm sure your snake will be fine. What's your name?"

Leila could think of nothing to say. It had been a long time since anyone had spoken to her. Her name might as well have been submerged in the bottom of a well, moored to an anchor. She couldn't seem to lift it up and out of her throat. So, she said nothing and felt better doing so.

"Ok. I understand. You're frightened. It's okay. My name is Darius. And that funny-looking guy driving with the crazy hair is Xavier. He's the one that found you and saved you from those mandrills. You're quite the brave one, aren't you?"

Leila waved her hand "hello". It was enough thanks for the two men who began to refocus their efforts on getting the child to safety.

"I've got some pills that might help ease your pain a little," Darius added, pulling out a bottle of ibuprofen. "Look, watch me. I will take one so you know it's safe." Darius stuck out his tongue and placed a single pill on it before swigging it down. He then showed Leila his open mouth to prove that he had indeed swallowed it. Darius' showmanship tickled Leila and she managed a small chuckle which greatly impressed him. He handed the girl two pills and a bottle of water. She gladly took both and finished the bottled water in one gulp. It didn't take long for Leila's pain to become much more manageable. After a short while, the bumps in the road were barely noticeable. She was even able to sit up with her legs outstretched on the back seat.

Xavier had driven them to a large village bustling with life. It was clear to Leila that the chaos of the collection hadn't reached the small town whose villagers seemed to go about their daily routines as they had always done. Seeing all the happy people in the town eased Leila's fears.

"Where are we?" she asked, peering out of the truck's window at all the activity.

"This is a small farming village called Tutu Town. You'll be safe here. Everyone knows each other. Tutu Town's tribes have been living in peace for more than a thousand years," Xavier said while looking in his rearview at Leila's reflection. "You're from South Africa, aren't you?"

Leila nodded her head in agreement. She smiled as Darius patted his friend on the shoulder for having guessed where the young girl was from on the first try.

"Where are your parents?" Xavier asked.

"Yeah, where's your mum and dad?"

"They're dead, I think. I don't know where they are," Leila said while her sad eyes focused on the streets of Tutu Town. The two men looked at each other and didn't ask any more questions of her.

The orange Land Rover pulled up onto a concrete pad next to a tiny white building with blue crosses painted on its facade. Leila knew the symbol meant that it was a hospital. The men carried her out of the truck and brought her inside the building through the back entrance. Once inside, they laid her down in an empty examination room which was nothing more than a cot surrounded by modular fabric partitions. The stiff cot was more of a bed than Leila had slept on in more than a month. Her body gladly settled onto its taut frame. She would have fallen asleep right then if weren't for the immediate care she was given. A tall, thin woman with a severe look and deep creases on her face, gave Leila a local anesthetic. She had the two men hold the girl down and then forced Leila's foot back into place. Even with the medicine, the readjustment hurt like hell. Leila screamed out while squeezing the crap out of Darius's hand. The tall woman bathed Leila's foot in a strong-smelling astringent and then wrapped it in gauze that had been dipped in a cloudy, oatmeal-like solution. The gauze dried instantly after it was applied and became rock hard. It was Leila's first cast and she was unusually proud of it.

"I'm sorry but she cannot stay here. You must find another place for her to rest. Take this. It is medication for the pain. Two pills twice a day with food," the woman said in a thick accent, a combination of Portuguese and a local African dialect. She thrust a small white envelope containing Leila's meds into Xavier's hand.

"Angela Tsahalo will look after her for us," Darius assured the woman. "Thank you so much for your help doctor." Leila was surprised to hear Darius address the woman as 'doctor'. She had thought the woman had been a nurse or something because she wore plain clothes. Leila then realized that there were no nurses. The hardworking doctor had no one to help her. She was the only person in the little hospital and many people were calling on her.

"Yes. Ms. Tsahalo is a very kind woman. That is a good place for her. Make sure she drinks plenty of water and gets something to eat. Grab a pair of the wooden crutches by the backdoor on your way out." The doctor nodded her head in approval and walked off to attend to her other patients.

Darius scooped Leila up into his arms and brought her out to the Land Rover while Xavier grabbed the crutches. Soon they were bouncing up and down a bumpy road that led them away from the village.

"Where are we going now?" Leila asked, feeling more at ease but still a little anxious.

"We're taking you to Angela's house. She is a very kind woman who we hope will agree to look after you until you get better," Xavier answered while driving.

"She has a small cottage on the middle of that hill," Darius said as he pointed to a hillside directly ahead of them.

"Why are there so many people here? None of them registered for the shelters?" Leila asked.

"Registered?" Darius laughed, "Most of these people don't even own televisions or computers. How would they have heard about it?"

"They don't have cell phones? Everybody has cell phones. I saw a picture of an Eskimo with a cellphone once," Leila reasoned.

"Yes, they have mobile phones but no internet. There are many villages like this all over the world," Xavier added. "There are millions of people who have been left out of the collection. All the big cities, like Johannesburg and Cairo, are deserted. But not these places."

"Why didn't the two of you go underground? How did you know not to?" Leila asked.

"Same as you. We didn't want to go. We thought we'd take our chances on our own," Darius replied.

"No, you don't understand. My family and I registered in Johannesburg."

At this Xavier stopped the car immediately. He looked at Darius with a look of total surprise.

"What did you just say?!" Darius exclaimed turning around in his seat to face the young girl, "You registered?"

"Yea, it was horrible. I mean, it *is* horrible."

"Wait! Then why are you here? Why aren't you still in the shelters?"

"I was freed. I mean, I was allowed to leave." Leila assumed the men knew nothing about the lizard people from below. Judging by the two men's reactions, she was right.

"Freed? What exactly is going on down there?"

"The government lied to everyone. There are no storms. The people down there are dying. The shelters are prisons."

"Prisons?" Xavier asked.

Leila told them a shortened, PG-rated version of what had happened to her, careful to leave out talk of the reptilians. She didn't want her new friends to think she was crazy just as her mother and father had. The guys sat in their seats completely mystified. They didn't know what to say.

Xavier started the truck again and drove uphill toward Angela's home. Darius cleverly put on some music so that he and Xavier could have a private conversation. They had to consider the implications of Leila's story. They soon reached Angela's home. It was a humble clapboard bungalow that stood alone, surrounded by the most beautiful flora. They parked the Land Rover next to a wild berry bush and Xavier got out to announce their arrival by knocking on the front door of the house. A large woman wearing a red and white striped bandana with a blue and white polka dot summer dress came to the door. She spoke with Xavier before the two of them walked back toward the SUV. The woman opened the back door and looked at Leila up and down in disbelief.

"Little girl, what is your name?"

"Leila."

"Okay, Leila, please come. You will stay with me. Come on." Angela was as strong as an ox. She picked Leila up just as Darius had done and brought her up the porch steps and into the house. Darius and Xavier followed but only to say goodbye. They promised to return in a few days to check on the young girl's recovery. Leila thanked them for saving her and watched as the bright orange Land Rover drove down the hill and away from the house until it was completely out of view.

"I have an extra room for you. It is the same room that I let my sister use when she comes to visit. You can sleep there." Angela helped Leila into a sunlit room decorated with maps glued to the walls that gave them the appearance of wallpaper. There, as bright as a cloud on a spring day, sat a clean bed with four fluffy white pillows. Angela peeled back the blankets and tucked Leila in careful not to disturb her injured foot.

"You must rest. Sleep as long as you like. When you wake, I will feed you red bean soup."

"Thank you," Leila mumbled. She was already asleep by the time Angela closed the blinds over the one large window. The woman gazed upon the child's sleeping face with earnest compassion then quietly closed the door behind her as she left the room.

CHAPTER THREE

The Door

Nick drove past the fire road that led to Tommy's cabin. He was scouting for soldiers or anyone who might have responded to Dale's broken tablet or the reptilian's death. He patrolled the entire town in search of signs of the military but there wasn't a soul in sight. He was well aware that it had only been a couple of days since he and Tommy had left which was all the more reason to be cautious. There was a good possibility that when he returned to the cave there would be specially trained soldiers lying in wait for him. He knew the military's protocols for 'snatching and grabbing' all too well. But his mind was made up and his heart had accepted the terms of engagement. Nick made an abrupt U-turn and headed back toward Tommy's cabin. The fire road was empty and quiet. He decided to check the cabin first before heading to the mine. There might be evidence of a presence having been there. The closer he came to it the slower he drove. Nick wasn't surprised at what he saw.

Someone had blown a man-sized hole through the garage door. Complete overkill, Nick thought as he parked his truck on the gravel driveway. The ex-soldier got out and quietly strapped on a bulletproof vest and then took out his shotgun from the toolbox that straddled the bed of his truck. Nick took his time surveying the perimeter. He wasn't about to be taken off guard again like he had been by the toe-headed biker from the airfield.

Nick crouched down and searched the exterior of the house looking for trip wires, well-hidden cameras, or any signs of a trap. He found nothing. He slid into the cabin through the back door that led to the kitchen and stormed into every room of the house. Things were just as they had left them. It was time to check the garage. The damage done to it, in Nick's mind, could be only one of two things: desperate looters looking to score or a clever attempt at making a sophisticated breach look like the work of desperate looters. Seeing as how nothing in the main part of the house had been disturbed Nick was leaning toward the latter interpretation. Nick flashed his Maglite into the garage and entered inside. The felt-lined table that once sat more or less in the middle of the garage had been overturned forcibly, most likely from the same explosion that blew a hole in the garage door. The cellar door had been swung open hard. It hung loosely by its top hinge. Nick crept down into the cellar to investigate. The large lids that covered the earthen refrigerators had all been left open. He checked inside each one. He knew the body of the lizardman would be gone. It was. Someone or something had taken it. Tingles went up Nick's spine as he ran out of the garage and back to his truck. The fact that the creature's headless body had been removed was evidence enough for Nick's suspicions to hold up. His heart began to race and all he could think about was Tommy's warning. He knew his best friend was right. Going into the mine, at this point, was suicide. The mine would, no doubt, be refortified somehow. He wondered if he would encounter human resistance or find more vicious beasts inside.

Nick fired up his truck's engine and drove down the dirt road toward the mine. He was determined not to let fear impede his desire to know the truth. He took a sharp left up the embankment that led to the mine's entrance. The mouth of the cave had been boarded up with freshly cut 1"x4"s. More evidence that he was on the right trail. Nick geared up and loaded his rucksack with everything he would need to open the mysterious portal. He pried the boards from the entrance and stacked them neatly to one side then pushed forward into the mineshaft. There was no need to check on Dale's rotting corpse. It had most likely been moved along with the reptilian. Nick went straight for the door, the same door that had been nagging at him for the last three days. The sense of anticipation overwhelmed him. He slowed his breathing and focused on the steady beating of his heart.

Nick navigated the last tunnel leading to the giant door, but as he turned the corner, he stopped. He couldn't believe his eyes. The massive door had been opened. Someone or something had left it slightly ajar. Natural light from the other side of the portal poured into the cave illuminating the area around its threshold. Nick lowered his optics to scan for thermal signatures but saw nothing of interest. He shook his head in confusion. Something was wrong. He was sure that whoever had left the door open was most likely waiting for him on the other side. Nick cautiously approached the huge circular hatch and kept his eyes peeled for tripwires or creases in the dirt where pressure plates might have been buried. Just as he was about to pass through the door Nick heard the distinct click of a round being chambered. He whirled around to survey the tunnel behind him. It appeared empty. That's when a single shot went off. A lone bullet tore straight through his thigh dropping Nick's left leg to the ground. BAM! Another bullet whizzed through the air grazing Nick's gun arm causing his weapon to fall to the floor. Nick was being shot at but couldn't tell where the bullets were coming from. Through the pain, he trained his eyes on portions of the tunnel's walls that had begun to move toward him. What he was perceiving didn't add up. He must have been witnessing a new kind of security system. Finally, from the middle of the tunnel, three soldiers removed an advanced kind of body armor from over their heads, yet their bodies remained invisible somehow. He hadn't seen the men at all even though they had been hiding in plain sight. Nick cursed aloud. He realized he would never get the chance to see what was beyond the door. The soldiers closed in on him and Nick did the only logical thing: he surrendered. He lay down on the ground and interlocked his fingers behind his head. One of the soldiers closed in and knocked Nick out cold with the butt of his rifle.

When Nick came to he was on his knees. His hands were zip-tied behind his back and there was a sack over his head. The sound of combat boots thundering toward him caused Nick to brace himself for another blow that didn't come. Instead, his bonds were cut and the bag over his head was removed. The pain from his bullet wound came on full force. Nick quietly groaned as he looked around. They were in an enormous underground military bunker. The bunker's fifty-foot walls had been machined smooth and branched into a vast array of tall corridors that stretched out as far as the eye could see in every direction. Nick turned his head toward the six soldiers who were standing in a firing squad formation, their rifles converging on him. The soldier that had freed Nick threw him a garment sealed in plastic along with a clear tube of blue metallic liquid on the ground by his side.

"Take off your clothes. Squeeze the liquid bandage onto your wounds and put the clothes in the bag on now!" The soldier had a rough Slavic accent. Nick did as he was told and stripped down to his tighty-whiteys. He applied the strange ointment to his wound. It felt cool against his flesh like toothpaste. As the gel hardened it released a numbing agent which lessened the pain considerably. Nick had never seen the military grade dressing but, whatever it was, it worked like a charm. He put on the clothes that were folded neatly inside the plastic bag. It was nothing more than a glorified hospital gown. He exhaled deeply in frustration while waiting for further instructions. He didn't understand why he was even alive.

"Get up, turn around, and walk straight ahead. Go. Now!" the soldier commanded.

Nick obeyed and walked straight toward what appeared to be a dead end. Confused, he looked back toward the soldiers. He lifted his arms as if to question their reason for having him walk into an empty bulk-head. Two of the men fired warning shots at Nick's heels in response to his hesitation. He dared not look back again. Nick reached the dead end and impatiently put his hands on his hips.Were they going to execute him, he wondered? His mind raced through all the crazy things that had happened to him in the last few days when the floor underneath him suddenly gave way. Nick slid down a highly polished system of tunnels. He tried stopping himself but there was nothing for him to grab onto and the shaft was too wide to flail his limbs out like a spider. After falling for what seemed like an eternity, Nick was finally ejected from the tunnel's opening. He rolled, end over end, out onto a hard, damp concrete floor. Dusting himself off, he got up and saw that he was in a large cell that looked like the cargo hold of a freighter. There were several hundred people inside the chamber. Its menacing red walls loomed over everyone like dark monoliths. The mass of human bodies made the dungeon humid and rank, a breeding ground for disease. His eyes darted, to and fro, as he searched the interior for any means of escape. There was a single door, identical to the one from the mine, on the far side of the chamber. The reptilians had to be involved with the place, he thought. The dungeon confirmed what Nick had already suspected. The U.S. military and the lizards were collaborating, but to what end?

Nick couldn't understand what was going on. He sauntered toward an empty section of wall and slumped down against it. He put his head, still throbbing from being hit by the butt of a rifle, in his hands. He had risked his freedom for nothing. He wasn't going to find any answers in a military-grade dungeon. As he sat there mulling over the reality of his situation, a voice spoke to him from the shadows.

“Welcome to hell,” an old man wheezed, looking at Nick through a mop of disheveled grey hair.

“What is this place? Please, tell me this isn’t a shelter,”

“More or less,” the old man laughed feebly, which, in turn, made him cough horribly. He spat phlegm onto the floor in front of them then turned his attention back toward Nick.

“What the hell is going on?”

“There ain’t enough food and water to go around. When the food does come those assholes over there in that corner take it all for themselves. I can’t remember the last time I ate. There aren’t no windows or clocks in here. It’s like a damn casino but without the pretty waitresses passing out free drinks. Time just seems to stand still in this place.” The old man pointed to a ring of spouts along a horizontal seam in the wall. Each spout was spread out twenty feet or so from the next. “The only clean water we get comes out those flanges in the walls. You’ll be lucky if you can muscle your way to one of ‘em to drink.”

“Holy Shit,” Nick gasped. Tommy had been right to harbor suspicions of the shelters. If only he could see them firsthand. It was way worse than Nick could ever have imagined. He wondered if the conditions inside the shelter were the same everywhere in the world. This was America, he thought. How could anyone do such a thing to citizens of the United States?

“I’m afraid that ain’t the worst of it. This place is run by demons. Well, nobody knows what the hell they are, but I do. Look close. Can you see the fear on everyone’s faces? It wasn’t put there by hunger or thirst, but by demons.”

“Demons?” Nick knew the man was talking about the lizardmen. But he wasn’t about to let anyone know he’d seen or killed one. “You do think you’re in hell, don’t you?”

“The Bible says this is how it’s gonna be in the last days. I just hope Jesus keeps up his end of the bargain.”

“Thanks. I appreciate the help.” Nick got up wanting better company even though he was grateful for the information the man freely gave.

At a loss for answers, Nick’s mind settled on the men who were controlling the food within the shelter. He looked over toward their small corner of the prison. He counted eight of them. Nick understood how the very few could keep the others, who far outnumbered the bullies, in check. He could see that the shelter was nothing more than a microcosm of society. A book he had read about ancient Sparta came to mind. He remembered reading that the Spartans, who maintained a standing army of only 60,000 men, were able to control more than 350,000 slaves in mental and physical bondage through the strategic use of fear and intimidation. Nick clenched his teeth and began to walk directly toward the brutes in a foolhardy search for justice.

"Easy, Army," a low, soothing voice from behind Nick spoke, "those fellas have already killed five people. And, in here, when you're close to death, nobody helps ya cuz that's just one less mouth to feed."

"How did you know I was Army?" Nick asked, annoyed at having been stopped. The man's 'spot-on' observation made Nick curious and distracted him from his prior objective.

"C'mon, man. You've got your damn rate tattooed on your leg." The man reached out and pointed to Nick's tattoo. "Everybody calls me, 'G'. I used to be an air traffic controller on the Roosevelt before, well… before all of this." Nick shook his hand. G smiled revealing two gold-capped incisors. Nick looked down at his tattoo which was visible under the pale green hem of his medical gown.

"How'd you know about the tat?" Nick soured. He was in a foul mood. The stench, the bullies, the shelters, the whole thing was too much.

"My ex-girlfriend's pops has that same ace of spades tat. Whenever he got drunk he would ramble on about his glory days. You guys are called blackjacks, right? Some kinda special recon unit or somethin'."

"Oh yeah? What was his name?" Nick replied in disbelief. The ace of spades tattoo was a closely guarded secret within the brotherhood of operators he knew. It was a violation to break that trust.

"Brighton. David Brighton."

"Brighton? You know Dave! My God, really?" The mention of the man's name brightened Nick up considerably. Brighton was not the loose-lipped type. The fact that he would share anything with a sailor was proof that G was a stand-up guy. "Brighton was one of my mission evaluators. My name's Nick, Nick Camby. I'm sorry. It's the first time anyone has ever placed my rate. How long have you been down here?"

G shook his head, "Bro, do you see any clocks around here? How on God's green Earth am I supposed to know?"

"Have you ever seen anyone leave? There's got to be a way out of here." Nick wondered aloud as his eyes furtively bounced around the room. G shook his head again.

"No. No one gets out. I think that's the whole point. Anyway, if I were you, I wouldn't sweat those dudes in the corner. You got something else comin' that I guarantee is a whole helluva a lot worse."

"You mean the 'demons'?" Nick made quotation marks with his fingers, "Yeah, I know about 'em already."

"Well, okay, hotshot, but don't let one of 'em eye you because I've seen 'em mangle three times as many people as those fools in the corner. They're due to come in here any minute now, too. We haven't had a food drop-off in a while. When they do come, I suggest you do what everyone else does and make yourself scarce. That is unless you want to die." G looked at Nick with a deadpan smirk.

"What's that big hole in the middle of the floor for?"

"That's the head, homie! Don't fall in," G toyed with him as he began to walk away. "One last thing, Army. When the water comes, you'll feel it first in the walls. Get to one of those holes before anybody else if you want to survive."

G walked off to chat it up with some other people while Nick sat back down against a wall, stowing the intense emotions that were roiling in his stomach. He continued to observe the brutes with keen interest. As Nick searched his own emotions, he came to realize the focus he was giving the bullies was his way of dealing with the uncertainty of the shelters and their true purpose. His gut told him to be patient. An opportunity would arise- a moment where he would be able to change the environment of the shelter for the better would present itself.

An unknowable amount of time passed. Nick was thinking about Tommy and Arnold when he felt a series of small vibrations coming from within the walls. Nick remembered what G and the old man had told him about the water. He looked up and saw that he was already seated directly underneath one of the waterspouts. Nick stood up just in time to catch a small rivulet of clean water in his mouth. He swallowed three mouthfuls before being pushed out of the way by a thirsty mob. Nick got as far away from the onrush as possible. The entire cell descended into chaos. People were slipping and falling all over each other. It was every person for themselves. Nick watched the brutes in the corner drink freely without being rushed. No one dared go near them or the flanges located within their small fief. After the flow stopped, many got on their hands and knees to lap up the remaining water as it drained into the hole in the middle of the cell. Nick watched in horror as an elderly couple, reeling from unquenched thirst, volunteer themselves into the gaping hole. They held each other's hands before disappearing beneath the rim of the pit. The ex-soldier ran over to them and peered down into the darkness but saw nothing but an endless cavity. Wretched smells rose from its depths and filled Nick's nostrils. He backed away in disgust. Nick surveilled the room looking for traces of empathy from the other prisoners. Barely anyone had noticed what had just happened. White-hot anger shot up inside Nick's heart. Utter complacency had always been America's worst problem, he thought. How could anyone sit by and let such dreadfulness ensue without standing up against it? Nick still believed in life, liberty, and the pursuit of happiness. He still believed America was worth dying for even though it appeared that he was alone in his convictions.

Whoever designed the shelters made death a constant and imminent threat. If one didn't starve, there was dehydration. There were also bullies, reptilians, and the silent killer, disease, all of which could spell an end to one's life. The more Nick thought about the shelters the more he became convinced they were a malicious experiment. If this were indeed the case then somewhere inside the prison were cameras documenting everything that was going on. Nick searched every section of the cell like a madman for evidence of surveillance equipment. Finally, something caught his eye. On the upper portion of the shelter's walls, some ten feet above his head, a grouping of beveled panels lorded over everyone below. The panels' texture and color matched the interior walls perfectly, but it was clear they were made of a different kind of material, most likely acrylic. Nick had originally assumed the panels were simply a design element. But why would anyone create designs in a prison unless they served a purpose? No, their placement had been strategic. From the vantage point of the panels, Nick surmised that almost every angle of the prison could be monitored. He racked his brain to the point of exhaustion in hopes of cobbling together a logical explanation for everything he and his fellow Americans were experiencing to no avail. Nick decided to get some rest. He had to turn his mind off for fear of losing it altogether. The ex-soldier curled into a ball on the damp cold floor wanting nothing more than a hot shower and a warm blanket. He closed his weary eyes hoping for a dream that would take him beyond the walls of his confinement.

∞

Nick's runaway emotions eventually leveled out. The shock of being incarcerated under false pretenses faded. Nick became fascinated at how plastic people were. The cell and its inhabitants were living proof that you could stretch the human psyche considerably before breaking it completely. He was still trying to come up with ways to escape; most of them centered on the food drop which still had not come. He wished Tommy was with him. His genius would've figured out a way out. But, then again, Tommy was smart enough never to have ended up in the shelters to begin with.

Nick learned that everyone's families had been split up except for mothers and their infants. He tried to imagine the grief of parents whose children had been taken from them. For that reason, Nick began to take a special interest in the children of the cell. They didn't know it, but Nick watched over them. He made sure they weren't in danger of being abused or worse. Something had to be done to establish order and civility among everyone. Nick continued to wait for such an opportunity. And while he waited, he was forced to confront the many unexamined issues in his own life; issues he'd been sidelining for years. Nick's mother had died while giving birth to him. His only memory of her came from the few dusty photographs his father had kept around his childhood home. His father unapologetically blamed Nick for the death of his one true love. He, too, died without ever forgiving his son. The festering guilt and pain gripped Nick's heart like an iron maiden. Still, Nick loved his father but when his ex-wife, Victoria, died he felt cursed. Since that time,

Nick had failed to accept responsibility for the man he had become and, consequently, developed many of the same self-destructive tendencies as his father, especially when it came to drinking. The brutality of the shelters caused Nick to wake up from his entrenched self-denial. Unfortunately, overwhelming hunger pangs prevented him from completing the process of healing.

Finally, the loud screech of the metal door being wrenched open signaled to everyone that it was time to hide as best they could. Nick watched as scared people scurried every which way cowering in the corners of the shelter like cockroaches in the light. G ran up to Nick and nudged him in the side.

"Yo, Army! This is it. This is what I was talking about. Just wait 'til you see these things, man. You should back up. You don't want 'em lookin' at you." G was anxious and kept his knees bent ready to retreat further back into the shadows if necessary. But the sailor didn't know that Nick had a plan which was fueled by a burning desire to make a difference in the lives of his fellow Americans. Instead of fading into the background like everyone else Nick stood with his back straight and waited for his moment to tip the scales.

A thundering roar rang out into the cell. The frightening sound reverberated against every wall. All the prisoners shuddered at once, cowering at the arrival of the lizardmen. Nick looked over at the alpha males in the corner. They were well hidden in their shadowy alcove. Nick understood perfectly why the brutes had picked that spot and never moved from it. It was almost completely out of view from the entrance to the cell. Nick turned his attention back to the four 'demons' that had walked inside. Two of them carried a litter packed with MREs while the other two stood guard by the door in case any-one tried to make a run for it. The creatures stood seven feet tall and were all elaborately colored just like the one Nick and Tommy had killed.

The imposing lizardmen set the litter of food onto the floor of the cell but did not immediately leave. They prowled the shelter showcasing their dominance and looking for anyone stupid enough to challenge their authority. This was the exact moment Nick had been waiting for. He started to run toward the center of the cell. G tried to hold him back but Nick yanked his arm away and gestured for G to keep quiet. Nick took one last deep breath and, to everyone's horror, started waving his arms wildly and cursing up a storm.

"Hey, lizard brains, over here you ugly sons of bitch-es! Yeah, that's right, over here! C'mon! What are you waiting for? I'm not scared of you!" Nick beat his chest like a gorilla as he yelled at the top of his lungs, "you guys look like a bunch of oversized chicken nuggets to me!" The serpent warriors' eyes flared and three of them charged after the insolent prisoner. Nick made a bee-line to the alcove where the brutes congregated. Seeing that Nick was coming their way they desperately scrambled to repel him, but it was no use. Nick had catapulted himself off the arched back of some cringing coward and had landed on top of the shoulders of the alpha males who were trying like the dickens to grab him. Nick expertly hoisted himself up into the upper corner of the brute's alcove which had an odd L-shape to it. He held himself aloft and out of reach of the men below using every bit of strength he had. His fingers had luckily found a thin edge of a seam in the wall helping him to maintain his strenuous position. The maneuver was a success. After having followed Nick, the lizardmen began tearing apart the biggest men from the group of bullies. The brutes fought back as best they could but they were no match for the ferocity of the reptilians whose claws ripped apart their soft, plump flesh easily. Shrill, blood-curdling screams charged the atmosphere of the shelter as people witnessed the unbridled strength of their captors on full display. When the guards had finished they left six bleeding human carcasses where they lay for everyone to see. To Nick's surprise, one of the reptilians returned to the scene and probed its head further into the tiny niche where the ex-soldier was hiding. The creature saw him, but instead of attacking it narrowed its eyes and smelled the air around him. Nick couldn't hold himself up for very much longer. The sharp pinch of his liquid bandages ripping off his skin, caused by the enormous stress he was putting on his leg muscles, was quickly becoming unbearable. Beads of sweat that had dripped down his arms had reached his fingertips, weakening the integrity of his grip on the narrow seam. Thankfully, the reptilian's commander ordered the guard to return to the hatch. And, just as the door to the shelter slammed shut, Nick fell to the ground on top of a heap of bloody dismembered bodies. He exhaled deeply but there was no time to waste. The ravenous appetites of the people were just about to ruin Nick's entire plan. He jumped to his feet and ran over to the pile of MREs pushing people out of the way and shouting at the top of his lungs.

"Stop! Stop it!" Nick cried out as loud as he could while thrusting himself between the prisoners and the target of their rabid hunger. "G, where are you?" he called out for help. There was no way he could hold off as many people as were waiting to eat. They gave Nick pause only because they had all seen what had just happened to the men who, for so long, had made their lives that much harder to endure.

"Right here, bruh." G came to the fore giving Nick props for what he had just accomplished. In the entire time G had been in the shelter he had never seen anyone handle it with the bravery and cunning Nick had. "You are one crazy mofo, dawg. I can't believe you just did that!"

"You've been here a while, right?" Nick asked. G nodded his head in agreement. "Choose ten people that you trust and make sure they're strong." G walked the cell and pulled out six men and four women whom he knew to be somewhat trustworthy. He brought them back to where the food was piled high. Nick looked approvingly at the ten people G had chosen then addressed everyone.

"These people are now in charge of who gets what in here. The new rules are very simple. Children and mothers with infants eat first. The elderly eat second. One food package to a person! There is enough to go around so there's no need to be rude. We will eat last. This new method of distribution is not open for discussion. This is how we are going to do things from now on. No more fighting over food. When it comes to water, well, just try to be nice to each other. But this is how we are going to conduct ourselves during food drops from now on! Understand? Good."

Heartfelt applause filled the stale air of the shelter. People cheered as they did their best to line up accordingly. There were a few arguments and shoving matches but Nick was unconcerned. He wasn't seeking to control, he was only seeking justice. As long as the elderly and the young ate first, Nick didn't care about everybody else. Nick stopped for a moment and noticed something was off. The old man who had spoken with him when he had first rolled into the shelter hadn't gotten in line. He was sitting off on his own, clearly unwell. Nick grabbed two MREs, sacrificing his own, and walked over to him tossing the food packs into his lap. The man smiled and dipped his chin. It was an unenthusiastic response, to say the least, but Nick could tell the man was grateful. After everyone had eaten people from all over the cell came up to Nick thanking him for what he had done. Nick was pleased with his actions. Their outcome had been the exact thing he knew everyone needed. The nature of the prisoners changed and they began to remember they had once been citizens of the mightiest country on earth.

CHAPTER FOUR

Surprise

Brandon was awakened by an unbroken tone coming from inside the drone's compartment where he lay. He slammed his powerful fist against the interior of the cabin to shut the sound up. He threw off the strap that held him while grabbing his aching head with the palm of his hand. Suddenly, the drone's compartment depressurized, and the lid opened automatically. Fragrant, humid air rushed in pulling with it diagonal sheets of drizzle. Brandon rolled out of the drone wanting nothing more than to get away from the monotonous tone drilling a hole through his head. The aircraft's lid closed as it rose from the ground before jetting off into the low-hanging clouds overhead. Brandon was angry. What kind of birthday present involved being marooned on what appeared to be a deserted island? Brandon wanted to get out of the rain and began walking toward the base of a lone mountain he hoped might have a few caves in it.

The drizzle continued to fall. It coated Brandon's skin in a thin layer of salty grime. He stopped underneath the splayed fronds of a palm tree to escape the rain and gather his thoughts. His instincts were telling him to get to higher ground so he could survey the island. But as his mind cleared itself of the drugs given to him desperation set in. The drastic contradiction between the comforts of the Royal Meridian's presidential suite and the place where he now found himself heightened his sense of alarm. Something was wrong. What had his father done? Who was Mr. Olivier? There was nothing to help him connect the dots. Brandon was on his own.

Brandon kept walking toward the mountain trying to keep his expensive shoes from getting too dirty. He was in no way the outdoorsy type and preferred the creature comforts of luxury urban living. While on his way he spied freshly made footprints in the mud. His heartbeat sped up as he realized that he was not alone. For some reason Brandon didn't try following them. Instead, he kept walking on. Wearing a five thousand dollar dolphin grey suit Brandon pushed past the water-ladened overgrowth. With every hard-fought step, the young man became angrier and angrier with his father. Brandon assumed that everything that was happening to him was nothing more than a cruel joke designed by Charlie to teach him a lesson in humility.

The hopeful heir had put a fair amount of distance between himself and the airfield when he heard voices off to his right. Brandon was surprisingly grateful to hear the casual chatter of a few grown men speaking English. He followed the voices until he came upon a group of five other young men huddled around a large black shipping crate. They were all soaking wet and, by the looks of it, had all suffered a fate similar to Brandon.

"Who are you? What the hell is going on? Where are we?" Brandon peppered the men with questions.

"You must be Brandon Tsang," said a slender man with a British accent.

"How do you know my name? Do you work for my father?" Brandon yelled. The men just chuckled, unmoved by Brandon's bravado. The Brit pointed to the shipping container prompting Brandon to walk over to it and take a look. Inside were nine metal cases each bearing an engraving of a different name. There was only one with a Chinese surname, his own.

"We can't open them. They've been set with some kind of electronic security system," another man said. "Allen Davis," the American stood up to shake Brandon's hand.

"Brandon Tsang," he answered, making the rounds.

"Thomas Staffordshire," the Brit provided.

"Ahmed Mahmoud."

"Robert Mbongwe."

"Wait a minute. Is your father Sharif Mbongwe of Syntecha Industries?" Brandon asked.

"Yes, he is."

"What about the rest of you? What businesses do your families operate?" Brandon wanted to know. He sensed a pattern forming and if his intuition was correct all of the men would be related to powerful captains of industry.

"My father owns a ship-building company in Oman," Mahmoud said, catching on to what Brandon was insinuating from his line of questioning.

"My grandmother owns the controlling interest of BioGen." Staffordshire added, "Europe's largest pharmaceutical research firm."

"My family owns the rights to most of the oil reserves in Alaska," Davis admitted, "What does your family do?"

"We own the first private bank in China among other interests," Brandon answered proudly. "What have you been told is going on?"

"It doesn't matter now, does it? We're here and by the looks of it, we've got no other choice but to wait for the others to arrive," Staffordshire said with a healthy dose of sarcasm.

"What do you mean 'it doesn't matter'? I was told I was going on a short vacation as a birthday present."

"Happy birthday," Mbongwe chortled. Everyone laughed at Brandon who didn't find any humor in the joke.

"I was supposed to be taking a private jet to meet an investor," Mahmoud provided.

"I was on my way to inspect semiconductors in Shenzhen," Mbongwe added.

"Who was the first to arrive?" Brandon asked. Mbongwe raised his hand.

"I arrived yesterday morning. I have been to the top of the mountain and have seen the layout of the island. There is nothing else around here, not even another island. There are no buildings. I stopped here after stumbling upon the container. When I saw my name inside along with others I knew that eventually, everyone would come."

"Why not wait by the airfield?"

“It is much drier here. The heavy rains will come again. Besides, the container is heavy. One person cannot move it by themselves.” Mbongwe answered Brandon who finally took a seat among the rest of the men.

They sat together at the foot of the mountain waiting for the other four men to arrive. Several hours after Brandon had settled in, a Japanese man named Akiro Watanabe arrived. Watanabe’s father owned the company that provided Japan with most of its nuclear energy. Six hours after that, a Russian oil baron’s son named Peter Kolarov appeared. Then, a Mexican by the name of Victor Alvarez, son of the owner of the largest media conglomerate in Latin America, showed up. The last to arrive was a Dutchman, Joachim Speer, whose family owned the mineral rights to some of the largest diamond caches in South Africa.

Everyone whose name was listed on one of the cases was present. They were an impressive sampling of the world’s richest and most powerful progeny. Once all were gathered, the cases inside the container began beeping. The beeps grew in frequency the closer each man got to his respective case. Brandon was the first to pick his up. The oscillating tone sped up to a fever pitch which somehow caused the case to unlock. Sensing it was safe, the others followed suit until all were facing the contents inside.

Brandon knelt on a patch of wet grass and laid out the items on a low-lying stone to inspect them. Three glass vials of clear blue liquid held together by a thin nylon strap sat next to a chrome injection gun neatly sheathed in an elegant calf-skin holster. The men picked up and examined the vials. They were about to start questioning each other when a holographic image of a hooded man wearing a woven black mask appeared above the empty shipping crate. The hologram's voice had been digitally altered to make the person speaking unidentifiable. As the man spoke his head steadily rotated to address all who were present.

"You have all been sacrificed for the glory of the Order. Your lives as you knew them are over. Each and every one of you must now take the first step toward ultimate power. But, before any of you can receive the honor and the privileges associated with membership in our most sacred brotherhood you must first prove yourselves worthy.

Underneath this island lies a network of caves more ancient than the pyramids of Egypt. Inside lives a being of exemplary martial skill. You are to locate and destroy this beast of war. If you refuse or fail to hunt the beast it will begin to hunt you. I promise that unless you engage the creature directly in open combat, none of you will survive. You have exactly forty-eight hours from this moment to complete this rite of passage. Do not let fear rule over your hearts or cloud your judgment, my young disciples. Embrace your brothers in death and be strengthened by the bonds of battle.

All of you have been provided with a potent serum called Exo. A single dose of this substance will last up to twenty minutes depending on your level of exertion. Once the serum enters your bloodstream your body will become filled with the primal urge to kill. Take the ancient weapons stored inside this container and boldly go forth. Remember, the Order is an invisible eye that never blinks or sleeps but watches over every action, every decision you make. Now, go and earn your birthright so that you may lead humanity into a new age. The Age of the Order."

As the hologram flickered and dissolved, a tray on the bottom of the container slid open revealing a stack of steel shields and swords, each the same as the last. Brandon's eyes fell to the ground in confusion. He tried to remember any element of his conversation with Olivier that could shed light on what was happening. To Brandon's surprise, every man reached into the container and took up their arms without discussion. Brandon reluctantly did the same. The men holstered their injection guns while looking at each other with blank faces. Someone had to speak up. Someone had to lead.

"Two hundred meters up from the base of the mountain there is a large opening in the rock, big enough for a man to pass through," Mbongwe offered as he pointed toward the leeward side of the peak. "I saw it yesterday on my way down."

"Lead the way, mate," Staffordshire insisted, banging his sword against his shield.

"Wait! That's it?" Davis asked with a sardonic smile. "No plan, huh? We're just gonna march straight into a pitch black cave?"

"He's right. We need to make torches or something," Speer agreed.

"Which of us knows how to make a torch?" Kolarov asked with a laugh. "You are all acting like you know what is going on. What is this *Order*? Do any of you know?" Silence pervaded for a while until Alvarez chimed in.

"I know how to make a torch. And I know what the Order is."

"Well, speak up for God's sake!" Davis shouted.

"Why should I tell any of you anything?" Alvarez asked, walking away from the group.

“Look, we’re all going to have to work together if any of us want to leave here alive,” the Dutchman appealed to the Mexican who was now standing off on his own with his back turned on the group.

“Who needs that asshole? I know how to make a damn torch. It’s not rocket science.” Davis ribbed, not making the situation any easier.

“My uncle used to talk about a secret organization that controlled both the black market and the banking system,” Watanabe said softly. “He said that even some governments did their bidding. But I have only just now heard the name, the Order. There is no way to be sure they are one and the same.”

“Who gives a damn who they are? I just want to go home. Let’s make the damn friggin’ torches and when we’re done Shaka Zulu over there can lead us to the caves.” Davis snarked.

“I am not Zulu! I am Ashanti,” Mbongwe protested. He was livid but Mahmoud was able to talk the African down.

To everyone’s surprise, Alvarez had started breaking smaller branches he thought would be good for torch making. Without questioning him, the others followed suit while the disgruntled American leaned up against a rubber tree and lit up a Marlboro.

A small group formed under Mamoud's suggestion and went off in search of tree resin or sap. When they were gone Alvarez finally opened up about what he knew about the Order. Kolarov, Speer, Brandon, and Staffordshire all lent their ears eager to hear what the young man had to say.

"The Order worships the darkness in men's hearts. They take part in strange rituals that give them the power to control the world from the shadows by exploiting people through blackmail and deceit. I have seen the ceremonies with my own eyes. My father is one of them. He is a very sick man. I want nothing to do with him but it's too late. Look at all of us. We are here because our families are bound to the Order. They have sacrificed us. I am afraid we're all dead men."

Alvarez's words dropped on everyone like anvils. Brandon was having a particularly hard time believing his father could deliver him to such a grim fate so casually. His birthday present had been the single greatest act of betrayal any father could unleash upon their child. Speer and Kolarov went off to talk while Brandon, Staffordshire, and Alvarez stayed behind to console one another.

"It could be worse, mate," Staffordshire suggested. "We could already be dead. At least we've been given a fighting chance."

"You're quite the optimist," Brandon replied, amazed at Staffordshire's positivity. Brandon wanted to strangle someone. Images of Charlie's face laughing and drinking alcohol kept playing in his mind.

"Prepare yourselves for the afterlife. Don't fight it. In my country, many people die before their time. It is a way of life. I will go and pray to Santa Muerte. You should do the same," Alvarez muttered with his head down. He walked off past the container and out of sight.

"This will *not* kill me," Brandon assured himself while balling his fists together. He looked up into the tumbling sky as if destiny was calling out to him. He could feel his grandfather's raucous spirit rising from within him. Right in front of Staffordshire Brandon closed his eyes and repeated the mantra, "I will not die on this island."

"That's the spirit. Hell, I'm sticking close to you," Staffordshire insisted. "That sort of mojo's bound to rub off on me. Come on, now. Let's gather this wood and bring it over to the container."

Brandon helped Staffordshire haul the makings for the torches. They broke off any sprigs still attached and waited for the others to come back with the resin. Mbongwe, Watanabe, and Mahmoud returned shortly after with a bundle of leaves full of thick brown tree sap.

"Alright, we have enough to make at least twenty torches," Mbongwe said out of the corner of his mouth while chewing on a miswak. The men made quick work of readying the torches. Speer and Alvarez constructed a sling out of several of the men's undershirts. Brandon and Watanabe put all the resin-tipped torches into the sling, hoisted it up, and looked around at their fellow comrades. It was time.

"Lead the way," Watanabe suggested, looking at Mbongwe. He had bonded with the African while searching for tree resin. The two men both had a deep love of nature and their shared knowledge of tropical fauna had helped ensure the success of their search.

"Excellent idea, let's get out of this bloody drizzle," Staffordshire said, gritting his teeth. "It just makes you feel so dirty."

The men laughed at the Brit's comedic flair and then set off for the cave. Mbongwe in front and the rest of the group trailed solemnly behind. The motley crew's contemporary attire coupled with the shields, torches, and swords they were carrying made the men appear as though they had traveled back in time a thousand years. No one spoke during their ascent. It was as if they were all marching off to the gallows.

It took them a little over an hour to reach the mouth of the cave. The men gained a healthy respect for the difficulty of the terrain in the process. The island was much larger than it appeared from the base of the mountain. The cave's entrance was shaped like a giant fang, which some of the men interpreted as an omen of the danger they would soon face. They managed to agree on a system for using the torches, one in front and one behind. They would also intermittently drop a few unlit torches on the ground for their hopeful return. Mbongwe lit his torch using Davis's lighter then fearlessly led the way into the bowels of the island. The single column of men traveled a great distance, listening out for any signs of the beast's presence. The narrow tunnels eventually opened out onto a vast cavern covered in crystal stalactites. A large groundwater reservoir rested at its bottom. Its emerald green waters were warm and shimmered with an ethereal light.

"Bioluminescent algae," Watanabe observed with a keen eye. The beautiful light playing off the heavily contoured cave walls drew the men closer. They decided to take a short break to drink from the underwater lake. The war party whispered to each other about the nature of their intended target unaware that they were being watched. The very creature they had been sent to kill sat in the shadows absorbing their scent. Unafraid of the hunters, or their intentions, the beast let out a bone-chilling howl.

The beast's roar echoed throughout the cavern sending the men to their feet. They scrambled to light more torches and the hunt was on.

"What the hell kind of animal makes a sound like that?" Davis asked, visibly shaken. "I've hunted big game before, but I've never heard anything that even comes close to that."

"It wants to let us know that it's here. It's watching us now, whatever it is," Watanabe said as he gripped his sword, ready for battle.

"What do we do now?" Mbongwe wanted to know, ready to spring.

"We stick together. We have a better chance of tracking and killing it together than if we split up," Brandon proposed. His years of martial training had prepared him for a moment like this. Without the slightest hesitation, Brandon took his injection gun, loaded it, and shot the serum into the side of his neck. Within seconds, a surge of power filled him with the desire for confrontation. He felt invincible and urged his fellow hunters to join him in his bloodlust. The other men injected themselves and were soon chomping at the bit, ready to go. They answered the monster's call by beating their swords against the rims of their shields in a unified display of bravery. As their blood boiled Brandon, driven by pure instinct, stepped up and took point.

"Remember," Brandon roared, "stay together until we kill the damn thing!"

The war party shouted in unison and charged off into the darkness of the cavern. They covered tremendous ground forging ahead like a runaway train charging down a mountain pass. The deeper the men went into the network of passageways the worse the odor became. The flickering tongues from their torches turned bright green, an indication of high amounts of sulfur and copper in the air. They had finally reached the heart of the beast's den and could see evidence of its defecation along with the disemboweled, half-eaten carcass of an island boar.

"It must be close! We have invaded its lair!" Mahmoud shouted, "Come out!"

"Shh! It must know that we are he---" Mbongwe's body was violently lifted into the air and gutted from throat to groin. Blood splattered everywhere, extinguishing the torch he held in his hand. The African's wretched cries rang out inside the cave, whose undulating ceiling and bulging walls acted as amplifiers.

"Over there!" Kolarov yelled as he threw his torch in the direction of the carnage. Orange and green fire lit up the underside of the creature's massive flanks. Brandon laid his eyes upon what looked to be a half-man, half-lizard standing nearly nine feet tall. It had a powerful tail which it whipped around furiously making cracking noises against the rock walls. Brandon threw himself at the beast and stabbed it in its side. He drove his blade into the creature's torso until the hilt prevented it from going any further. The lizardman let out a shriek that pierced Brandon's ears. Brandon tried to yank the sword free but it wouldn't budge. The creature's muscular arm swatted at Brandon who expertly lifted his shield just in time. The tremendous force of the monster's blow sent Brandon's body flying across the span of the lair. The wind got knocked out of him after he hit the same wall that housed the entrance to the cave. Staffordshire, sensing his opportunity, rose up after dodging the swath of the lizardman's tail. He brought his blade down like a mighty hammer and hacked the reptilian's tail off at its base. The gutsy strike cost the Brit his life. The reptilian became so enraged by the act that it grabbed Staffordshire's head with both hands and squeezed until the Brit's skull cracked open like an egg. The creature then threw Staffordshire's headless remains at Davis before running into the midst of four men and trampling them underfoot. The beast leaped into the air and repeatedly pounced on top of their flailing bodies. Brandon could hear bones cracking over their wails of agony. Watanabe, who had nimbly rolled away from the beast's charge, sliced the tendons in the back of its legs causing the behemoth to fall to its knees. Alvarez, still on the ground after being trampled, drove his sword upward into the creature's groin. The lizardman roared again and clawed viciously at everyone around him. In the space of a few seconds, it had decapitated Watanabe, shredded Alvarez, and cut whoever remained on the ground to ribbons.

Brandon, Kolarov, Davis, and Speer were the only men left of the nine. The lizardman, feeling the odds shifting in his favor, picked up the dead men's shields and began hurling them at the remaining four men who did their best to dodge the deadly missiles. The musty den grew dark as the fading light of only one torch remained. Its greenish fire fought valiantly against the darkness. The creature, sensing the importance of the torchlight, tossed Mahmoud's dead body on top of it to smother its flame. But Mahmoud's luxurious garments were highly flammable. Their combustion lit up the hollows as though it were a summer afternoon. The men gazed at the reptilian for the first time in good light. It was covered in its dark blue blood as well as the blood of those it had slain. The beast's glowing yellow eyes made it look as though it had been conjured from the darkest corner of a child's night terror. The hulking reptilian gnashed its fangs and stuck out its wicked tongue taunting his enemies.

"Surround it! Don't let it escape back into the cave system!" Speer shouted. Davis, who had been hanging back waiting for his moment to engage, finally rushed the creature who lunged at him in return. Davis stoically stabbed at the lizardman's abdomen but his attacks proved useless. The reptilian gorged itself on Davis's jugular. Brandon realized in that terrible moment that the monster was enjoying itself. Wasting no time, the young man picked up a loose sword from the cave floor and threw it at the beast's neck. The reptilian heard the sword's approach and whipped itself around while holding Davis in his jaws using him like a shield. The blade thumped into the American's chest putting the poor man out of his misery. Brandon searched for another sword among the dead. Kolarov ran straight at the creature with his shield raised and yelling obscenities at his enemy. The lizardman punched Kolarov so hard that it broke the Russian's neck instantly and flattened the nose of his shield. Speer didn't waste any time and slashed at the beast's left arm slicing it open at the elbow and then aimed for its throat. His second blow danced off the beast's dense scaling. Speer managed to evade the creature's swift counters even at close range. As it was busy fighting off the Dutchman, Brandon flung another sword with as much force as he could summon. The lizardman, once again, faced the whirling blade at just the right moment. The blade thwacked into the creature's cranium and sprayed sheets of blue blood into the ether. In the blink of an eye, Brandon jumped onto the lizardman's chest and bashed the rim of his shield into the blunt edge of the stuck blade until it cleaved the reptoid's skull in two. The beast dropped to its knees and collapsed face forward onto the dirt floor. Clouds of dust swirled upward into the air covering the two lone survivors. Speer, taking no chances, began hacking at the creature's thick neck until he succeeded in severing its head. Much like a snake, the reptilian's muscles continued to contract on their own for a while and then gradually grew still. It was over. Their formidable enemy had managed to kill seven of them. Only Brandon and Speer endured. They were both covered in guts and trembling from the rush of battle.

Basking in the glorious victory over the most deadly adversary imaginable, the two men embraced one another while praising each other's efforts toward dispatching the reptilian. But when their warm bodies touched something unexpected happened. They paused momentarily while looking into each other's eyes. As the flames given off by Mahmoud's still-burning body began to dwindle, they kissed amidst the company of their fallen comrades. Brandon had never felt such joy. At that moment, he realized he had been caged in heavy chains by the tedious expectations of his family for his entire life. The two men journeyed back to the mouth of the cave, swimming in the springs of their triumph and mutual attraction.

Brandon and Joachim finally stepped out into the night and breathed in the salty tropical air. They had a great view of the island and quickly took notice of the black transport helicopter hovering above the grassy clearing where the drones had dropped them off. Brandon playfully injected another dose of the potent blue serum into his thigh. The Dutchman did the same sensing the onset of a race to the finish. Without saying another word, both of them bolted toward the helicopter. Their muscles flexed through their clothing as they forded creeks and vaulted over fallen trees. Brandon made it to the edge of the airstrip first but stopped to wait for Speer who wasn't far behind. Speer knew he had been beaten but as a joke kept running to the helicopter which had already landed. Brandon didn't bother catching up. He laughed while he tried to catch his breath. After a few moments of rest, Brandon started walking toward the helicopter but stopped halfway when he saw several men exit the aircraft with what looked like tranquilizer guns. The men shot Speer in his neck and caught the Dutchman's limp body just as it fell to the ground. Before Brandon could protest, two darts hit him in the thigh. He didn't fight it. He was extremely tired and as the sky above him blurred he wondered if he would ever see his comrade-in-arms again. Two men carrying a stretcher recovered Brandon's body and brought him onto the transport, which took off as quickly as it could. The helicopter's rotors chopped at the humid ocean air propelling the craft further and further upward. Soon, it had left the uncharted island far behind and, with it, Brandon Tsang's innocence.

CHAPTER FIVE

Tutu Town

Leila's body was weak. It took all of her strength just to sit up in bed. Her muscles hummed with a deep and soothing relaxation. It was her first proper rest in a long time. The pain from her dislocated foot reminded her of the string of events that had led her to Tutu Town. She looked around the small, bright room and thankfully saw that her meds along with a glass of cool, clear water were sitting on a bedside table next to her bed. She took her medicine and then waited patiently for the painkillers to kick in.

Soft blue shadows cast by the rubber trees standing guard outside her bedroom window played against the crisp white sheets of her bed. The comfort Leila felt was not simply a result of resting. She also felt safe. After the drugs started working Leila threw her covers off and brought her thin legs over the lip of the mattress. The polished wooden floor felt nice underfoot but her legs might as well have been made of JELL-O. Since she'd arrived she hadn't once gotten out of bed and was curious to see the rest of the house. Leila reached out for her crutches that rested against the wall by the bed. She fumbled around with them for a while getting the hang of them then hobbled into the living room.

Leila expected to see Angela milling around in the kitchen but there was no one inside. The young girl meandered about handling all the decorations in the home. Many strange objects were hanging on the walls including masks of ebony adorned with multicolored beads. Leila's heart skipped a beat when she saw a mask that looked like a dumbed-down depiction of a Setian. It was made of pale wood and looked very old. She observed its details for quite some time in silence. The mask effectively conjured the presence of the fearsome creatures. Many of the mask's features were similar to a real Setian: the placement of the eyes, the rounded protruding snout, and the elongated shape of the head. Leila wondered if Angela had ever seen a lizard person in real life. Her focus eventually turned toward all the photos Angela had in frames. The photos were everywhere. Some hung on the walls next to the masks while others rested on tables or shelves. In every photo, Angela's big-hearted smile was the center of attention. The stalwart woman was very popular with locals and foreigners alike. Leila was sure that some of the people in the photos were famous even though she didn't exactly know who any of them were.

Leila had to pee pretty badly. She searched the tiny house for the bathroom but there wasn't one inside. Leila heard the barking of a dog coming from behind the cottage. There was a backdoor but she didn't feel comfortable using it. Her mother had taught her never to go into a door that you haven't been invited through first. She used the front door instead carefully climbing down the four wooden stairs that descended from the rickety porch. As soon as she hit the ground a cute puffy white dog with a big smile and gray tail came up to greet her. She welcomed the attention letting the dog lick her all over her face.

"Don't let Shima kiss you, she likes to eat dried poop," Angela said as she came around from the back-yard. She was pushing an old-fashioned wheelbarrow that had been cobbled together with woods of varying colors. "My goodness, little girl. Do you know that you have been asleep for two days?"

"Two days?"

"Yes. Two whole days. You must need to use the bathroom, don't you?"

"Hehe, yeah, I do. Where is it? I mean, do you have one?" Leila didn't want to sound rude. It had been weeks since she'd had a conversation with anyone and her manners weren't the sharpest.

"Come, I will show you. But next time use the back-door. It will be easier for you. Come on, child." Angela leisurely walked the girl up the slope and brought her around to the back of the house. The backyard was an acre of terraced garden overrun by flowers, vegetables, and fruit trees of all kinds. The sight pleased Leila very much and the smells were amazing. The garden was such an affirmation of life. Angela led the little girl down a stamped dirt path that led toward a red wooden shed that had a small rodent skull affixed to the door. Leila looked at Angela uneasily.

"Are there any spiders in there?" she asked as she peered into the dark corners of the shed.

"No, I don't think so. I sweep it every morning. Go on," Angela smirked, getting a kick out of watching a city girl adapt to living in the country. "You will get used to it."

Leila sat down on a sanded wooden bench with a hole cut into the middle of it. The smell coming up from beneath the cutout in the bench was really gross but the outhouse was still way better than the shelters. She finished her business as quickly as she could, gladly getting the heck got out of there. Shima ran up to her sporting a silly grin and wanting to play. Leila picked up a broken tree branch that lay at her feet. She threw the stick as far as she could. Shima didn't even turn her head. She just stared blankly at Leila with her tongue hanging out of her mouth. Leila laughed and was about to open the back door when Angela yelled at her from the kitchen.

"Are you hungry?"

"Yes, ma'am."

"Good. Bring me two big yams from the pile out there. Do you see them?"

"Yeah." Did Angela not see that she had to use crutches? Leila tried to figure out how exactly carrying two yams was going to work. She lifted her t-shirt and tied the bottom of it into a knot. Then she grabbed two of the largest yams she could find from the sun-drenched pile and folded them within the fabric of her shirt. She brought them into the kitchen where Angela inspected them and then nodded her head in approval. The large woman beckoned Leila to come closer so they could prepare breakfast together.

"Do you know how to cook, Leila?"

"Just sandwiches and cereal."

"Well, in my house you will learn how to cook and do many other things too."

"Okay."

"I want you to peel those yams, wash them in that bucket of water there, and then cut them into big chunks for me. Can you do this?"

"Uh-huh."

Leila enjoyed learning new things, especially if the teacher was as kind as Angela. She carried out her instructions to the best of her ability. The task took her a little longer than usual because she had to hop around the short distances in the kitchen. When Leila delivered the peeled, washed, and diced yams to Angela she looked at them and smiled. The hefty woman dumped the yams into a large pot that was simmering on a gas range. Angela showed Leila which seasonings to use to flavor the yams: turmeric for a little kick and white pepper to bring out the natural sweetness. She had the young girl slowly stir the pot for a few minutes. Afterward, Leila ground beans that had been soaking all night into a paste and mixed it with butter and goat fat. They worked hard for another hour preparing their first meal. When they were done, they both sat down together at a small round table off to the side of the kitchen, underneath a breezy window. The breakfast consisted of steamed squash resting on a bed of red bean paste and yams which were glazed in brown sugar and butter. The food looked wonderful, but by the time Leila sat down to eat she wasn't hungry at all.

"Leila, why aren't you eating your breakfast?"

"I don't know. When I woke up I was really hungry, but now I'm not."

"Oh, okay, I know. This is a common problem for a cook. The smells of the food have filled you up, but Dr. Mebina said that you must eat. So, please, try to eat what is on your plate. It will help you to become strong."

"Can't I just save it for later?"

"Later? I do not have an ice box, Leila, and it is a bad thing to waste food. You must eat!"

Leila didn't talk back. She stuffed the mushy food into her mouth and was pleasantly surprised at how good it tasted. When they were both done eating they cleaned up the kitchen which took almost half as long as making the meal itself. Leila realized that 'country living' was a lot of work. She felt bad for having given her mother such a hard time about possibly living at her aunt's farm in Wales.

"I must go into town today. I think it would be good for you to come. You will not be able to carry anything but you can keep the ledger. Many people owe me things.

You can write down for me what I take and from whom. Can you do this?"

"Cool! Yeah." Leila was thrilled at the thought of going into town on business. The job of keeping Angela's ledger reminded her of the things her mother had her do whenever they went shopping.

"You must write in a clear hand so that I can read it and no one can dispute what you have written."

"I have good handwriting."

Angela gathered what was necessary for the trip into town. The pair of them locked up the house and then made their way down to a large tool shed at the front of her property. Angela opened its doors to reveal a brilliantly colored sky blue moto with three wheels and a wide cart attached to the back. She poured a mixture of oil and gasoline into the moto's tank and then had Leila, along with her crutches, sit in the back without a restraint, much to the young girl's delight. Before long, the two of them were motoring down the unpaved road leading into Tutu Town.

Many colorful people were walking on the road to the village. Some held large bundles on their heads and others pulled carts behind them. Angela knew every person along the way. She would say hello or wave to everyone as she passed them by. On several occasions, she stopped her moto and chatted briefly in a local dialect Leila could not understand. She suspected that many of the conversations were about her, as Angela would often gesture over to her now and then without looking.

They eventually reached the bazaar in the center of town. There were even more people than Leila had remembered seeing the first time Darius and Xavier had driven her through it. Hundreds of shoppers were busy haggling and stuffing their bags full of food and other goods. The open-air market took up the majority of the busiest intersection in town. Angela parked her motorbike at the corner of an intersection next to a delightfully aromatic melon stand. There, she talked with the owner who, unsurprisingly, was also a friend. The owner agreed to watch over Angela's moto while she gathered the supplies owed to her.

"The first place we must go I will collect five pounds of fava beans. Follow me," Angela stated as she handed Leila a pocket-sized notebook with a blunt red pencil stuck into its spiral binding. "I want you to write 'five pounds, fava beans, Mr. Oguidoula'. O-G-U-I-D-O-U-L-A. Next to his name write today's date September 23rd, 2025." Leila wrote the information down as neatly as she could but had to stop walking to do it well. When she was finished, Leila tried her best to catch up to Angela, who was speeding around the marketplace like a worker bee in a hive. The heavyset woman wasted no time chatting. She was all business.

Angela and Leila spent the rest of the morning collecting the goods owed to her. At each vendor, Angela had to argue to get a fair trade and if negotiations had gone well she would take the time to introduce the young girl as her new assistant. Leila had already written a dozen names in the ledger along with all the corresponding data. She learned that, because of the nature of seasonal harvests, not everyone's goods could be traded at the same time. That is why the ledger was needed. Consequently, a very complex but informal network of accounting fueled the entire place. Leila had never experienced anything quite like it and was having a blast interacting with so many diverse people. She had forgotten how much she enjoyed the company of others.

The wonderful smells of fresh, succulent fruit tickled Leila's taste buds. All of the hustling and bustling had sparked her appetite. She coveted the ripe mangos, guavas, and bananas that sat idly in the shade of so many of the little shops. Occasionally, some of the vendors would offer samples of their foods to showcase their quality. Leila took advantage and got the chance to try many new things, some outright disgusting and some downright heavenly. Her favorite was the dragon fruit. Its colorful skin was very unusual but it had a nice clean taste that was crisp and sweet. Angela tried to persuade Leila into eating dried centipede but the little girl drew a firm line in the sand. Angela's business at the market wound down and, on their last trip back to the moto, they ran into two familiar faces.

"Angela!" Darius exclaimed. He nudged Xavier who was busy inspecting the label of a bottle of white wine. Xavier turned around and was pleased to see Leila looking healthy and rested.

"Hi, Darius!" Leila beamed. Darius opened his big arms and hugged Leila around her crutches.

"How are the both of you?" Darius asked, petting the young girl on the head but addressing Angela. "Do you need anything?"

"No, thank you. We have too many things as it is. I am concerned that maybe I have not left any room for Leila," Angela said over her shoulder as she lifted the last of the bags of food onto her moto. Leila began helping Angela strap down the cargo with colorfully striped bungee cords.

"Well, why don't you let us have the honor of Leila's company for rest of the day?" Darius asked in the most delightfully pleasant manner. "We will, of course, return this lovely little girl to yours later this afternoon." Leila blushed. She had forgotten that she had never told Darius or Xavier her name.

Angela stopped and thought for a moment. "This is good, but you must bring her home before sunset. I do not want her out in the town after dark. Do you understand?" Angela replied sternly. She looked at Xavier for confirmation. The two men promised. "Good. We can have supper together. Make sure she drinks lots of water. Leila, is this okay with you?"

"Yeah! It sounds like fun."

"Okay. I'll see you at dinner. Have a good time and try to stay off of your foot, for a little while at least. I have already made you walk too much today, I think," Angela added, hopping on her moto and starting its engine. She waved goodbye and then melted into the ever-shifting kaleidoscope of the hectic marketplace.

"Hey, Leila, run into any more mandrills lately?" Xavier asked mockingly.

"No. Have you shot any lately?" Leila replied, giggling.

"Haha. Well done, Leila," Darius joked giving Leila a high five. "So, we are on our way to class. Do you know anything about martial arts?"

"I know Bruce Lee! My dad liked to watch old Kung Fu movies all the time, but I can only remember Bruce Lee. Oh, and Jackie Chan. I know Jackie Chan too!"

"Very good. We are on our way to teach a martial arts class. Interestingly enough, Bruce Lee used to study the very same martial art that I teach," Darius added.

"Both of you teach martial arts?"

"Well, Xavier helps me just like you helped Angela today. He is a very good student. And it is always the best students that make the best teachers, right?"

"Yeah, that sounds about right, I guess. But how do you practice killing people?"

"Whoa, hold on there. Martial arts is not about killing people, luv. Martial arts is about finding balance at all times and in all forms," Darius responded, taking on a very serious tone.

"Have you ever killed anyone?"

Darius thought for a second while looking at Xavier. He wasn't sure how to answer the question. It was so straightforward. There wasn't any way to answer it without being dishonest.

"I have had to protect myself and others at the cost of someone else's life. So, yes, I have had to use lethal force on more than one occasion, but I didn't enjoy doing it. I don't wake up in the morning and think to myself, 'Oh, who can I hurt today?'"

"Okay," Leila chuckled, "I wanna learn how to fight."

"Well, we practice a sacred martial art called Wing Chun," Xavier leaned in close to the young girl's face as he continued, "and it was invented by a woman."

"Really? That's so cool. I wanna see it. Do you do flips and stuff?"

"No, but would you like to hear the story of how it was created?"

"I think I already know the story!"

"Oh yeah? Why don't you tell us then?" Xavier replied with an equal dose of sarcasm.

"The man wanted the woman but she loved someone else. The man tried to force her to love him so she learned how to beat him up. The end." Leila guessed. The two men looked at one another in amazement. It was an extremely crude retelling of Wing Chun's origins but it was the truth.

"How do you know the story? It's never been explained in any of the Bruce Lee movies I've ever seen," Xavier replied.

"Because that's what always happens to women in ancient times."

"Huh, never thought of it like that." Darius scratched his head. "Well, aside from what you may know of the story, the martial art was actually developed by an abbess. She was meditating one day when she witnessed a nasty fight between a snake and a crane. And that's how she came up with Wing Chun."

"What's an abbess?"

"It's a female monk. Y'know, like the Asian guys with the bald heads and the orange robes," Xavier explained.

"What? She didn't have any hair? That's funny," Leila laughed. "So who won? The bird or the snake?"

"No, only the men shave their heads and no one knows who won the fight. I don't think that's the point. It was the interaction between the snake and crane that inspired the abbess."

"Oh," Leila didn't understand but acted like she did.

The trio came to a two-story beige building and went inside. It was a French dance academy, but there were no dancers, only a handful of young men stretching and talking. The temperature inside the school was nice and cool. Leila looked up and was surprised to see a handful of ceiling fans whirling away.

“There’s electricity in here?” she asked, twirling under the cool breezes. “I thought the government shut off all the power everywhere?”

“They did,” Xavier quickly answered, “but they also left everything behind. That’s why I am here in Tutu Town. I provide power for everyone in the village and, in return, I can live here eating and drinking whatever I want. Cool deal, huh? There’s running water here, too. We use gas-powered generators to provide minimal electricity and pump water to all the villagers living nearby.”

“You know how to do all that kind of stuff?”

“I have advanced degrees in both mechanical engineering and microbiology. So, yes, I know how to do lots of things.”

Leila was suddenly filled with hope. She was sure Tutu Town wasn’t the only city surviving with modern amenities. Leila pictured an entire world without the horror of the shelters. If only her mother and father had come to Tutu Town instead of registering, they would still be living together as one happy family. Darius grabbed Leila’s hand and introduced her to everyone in the class, eight in all, not counting Xavier. She took a seat on one side of the room and watched the martial arts clinic begin.

Much to Leila's surprise, there were no women in the class. She didn't understand how a martial art that had been started by a woman could have no female students. Right then and there she committed herself to learning everything she could about Wing Chun. As the young girl observed the bizarre, repetitive exercises used in the class, she began to pick apart the fighting system with a preternatural sensitivity. After an hour of sitting and watching, Leila rose from her chair and limped over to the middle of the class leaving her crutches behind. All the students were practicing in pairs. Their forearms were pressed together in a kind of game where knocking each other off balance seemed to be the goal. She barged in on the youngest pair in hopes of having a go at one of them. The boy she was 'pushing hands' with couldn't have been more than fifteen, but he was very quick. She lined up her feet shoulder width apart, like the others, and dropped her center of gravity as low as possible. She then let her body relax into position placing the majority of her upper body weight onto her hips. Arms bent, yet thrust outward, the two students pushed both of their elbows against one another. Through only the feeling interpreted by the minute flexing of their forearms and subtle variations in weight displacement, Leila began compromising her opponent's stance time and time again. Her bad foot didn't slow her down at all. Soon, the other students began to take notice. One student after the other asked to 'cut in' to put the little girl in her place. And one after the other they fell victim to the girl's knack for exposing vulnerabilities in their stances. Finally, Darius stopped training with one of the older pupils and walked over to Leila. He watched her very closely as she 'pushed hands'. He said nothing but made small adjustments to both Leila's and her opponent's stances. Darius explained that Leila's center of gravity was highly developed giving her increased stability. Leila wondered if her time suffering in the shelters had anything to do with her facility for the exercise. She was pleased with the attention she was receiving. Darius decided on the fly that the girl needed to be challenged by a more developed student and asked a young man, named Cecil, to step in and push hands with her.

Cecil was another fighter altogether. He was extremely well-grounded and markedly faster than the others. His movements were fluid, not jerky at all. Using only his elbows and twists of his wrists, he bested Leila at every turn. Xavier articulated what was happening saying that the girl's bad foot was preventing her from truly becoming rooted and thus slowing down the left side of her body. Leila tried her best against Cecil but it was clear she was no match.

Darius called for a break. Most of the students left the school to have lunch while a few others hung around and talked shop. After being congratulated by those who remained behind, Leila did as Angela had asked and sat down to rest her foot. Darius came over to the young girl, and with his trademark grin rushed her so fast that she almost fell over in her chair.

"Haha, you're a natural, luv!" Darius exclaimed. "I've never seen anyone take to pushing hands as fast as you have. Never!"

"Really? It's more fun than it looks. I like it," Leila said looking up at him. "But I thought you kicked and punched in Kung Fu? This is all you guys do?"

"No, not at all. I want you to imagine that every attack, no matter if it is with a gun, a kick, or a sword, creates a shape, a form if you will. That shape is made by the attacker's center of gravity, the ground plane, and whatever they discharge whether it be a bullet or a fist. In Wing Chun, we study the forms of attack so that we can analyze, neutralize, and terminate any manner of aggression."

"That's so awesome. I think I get it. So if you kick straight out at someone you become like a rectangle?"

"Close. You have to imagine that the shape or form is 3 dimensional, right?" Darius continued, "So, if you were to walk up to a solid rectangle that is about as high as you are tall and about the width of your own body, what would be the best way to knock it over?"

Leila thought about it, picturing it in her mind. "Well, I would move to the side and push it over. I wouldn't go straight at it."

"Very good, Leila. That's right. But it's infinitely more complicated than that. You see the shapes or forms never stay the same for very long. In fact, during a real fight, they change very quickly. You must constantly adjust your position to that of your opponent so that you are always within the threshold of engagement."

Darius could see that he was losing the little girl. He racked his brain thinking of a metaphor when a light bulb visibly went off in his brain.

"Okay, so you have a message to send to someone you love or hate, it doesn't matter. What is the best way to get the message to its recipient?"

"You send a text."

"Exactly! And notice how the distance does not determine the logic of expediency. What I mean is, it wouldn't matter if your friend was next door or lived in Russia, text messaging is still the quickest method of sending it, right?"

"Yeah, of course!"

"And you would never send a letter to someone who lived next door to you, would you? I mean, if it had to get there as quickly as possible."

"No, that's stupid."

"See, in Wing Chun, a good practitioner wants to find the quickest, most efficient method for disabling their opponent. There are no flashy kicks. We get up extremely close to our opponent so their range of attack is limited and then we take them out."

"But that sounds dangerous."

"All fighting is dangerous, Leila. But what is even more dangerous is not knowing how to respond properly in a given situation. By concentrating on disabling the forms of combat you will become very good at anticipating a form's combat evolution or flow. And when you have been studying as long as I have you can easily determine what an opponent's next move will be just like in chess."

"I just don't see how you can do all that by just pushing your elbows together all the time," Leila said honestly.

"I know it looks odd to you now but this is the way Bruce Lee learned. This is the way Wing Chun has been taught for more than two centuries. Pushing hands trains your nervous system to respond, not just to the visual representation of your opponent's attack, but, to its inherent physical structure. That sensitivity is developed over years of training and I can assure you its application is most lethal when pitted against any other fighting system."

"I like it when you talk about Wing Chun," Leila gleefully admitted. "You're so passionate about it. I wanna learn too. Will you teach me?"

"What do you think I'm doing?" Darius replied. "You will be my next prized pupil. But to be my second-in-command you will have to beat Xavier. And I warn you he is strong and very clever."

"But I thought since women invented it that strength didn't matter."

Darius couldn't believe how tuned in the girl was. He smiled and put his hand on her tiny shoulder. "Stay off your foot for the rest of the day. If it's okay with Angela you can come whenever you'd like. We train here every day."

Leila sat down. Darius's mention of her foot caused it to ache even more. She wanted to heal quickly so that she could start learning how to fight. She wanted to be confident and powerful: everything she hadn't felt inside the shelters. Leila started to believe Wing Chun could provide a way for her to never feel afraid again.

The end of the class came and the warm afternoon sun drained into an evening sky. Xavier looked at Darius and pointed to his digital wristwatch. It was time for them to take Leila back to Angela's. They locked up the martial arts studio and jumped into the Land Rover. On the way to the cottage, Xavier pointed out the diesel generators used to power the town. He tried to explain the complex tolerances and pressures to Leila, but he might as well have been speaking Latin. They pulled up to the white cottage just as the sun was dipping below the horizon. The smell of food drifted out of the open windows of the tiny home and made its way down to the truck. Leila's tummy growled. She was having so much fun she hadn't realized how hungry she had become. The two men helped the little girl into the house and the four of them sat down together in Angela's living room. They ate heartily and shared stories well into the night. It was hard to believe that they all had met only a few days prior. Leila felt at home among her new friends. Her first day in Tutu Town had been nothing short of magical.

CHAPTER SIX

Death or Dishonor

The shelters had maintained an equilibrium of positivity ever since the alpha males had been slaughtered by the reptilian guards. Another food drop had come and gone and the order that Nick helped establish had survived the test of time. The people in the shelter were beginning to use their smarts by taking old empty MRE packages and storing water in them, greatly reducing sickness and disease. Now that the pressure to drink from the spouts had been mitigated, the citizens decided to delegate two waterspouts to bathing and washing gowns. Consequently, the stench of the dungeon lessened tremendously. Everyone had started to think beyond their immediate circumstances. Nick even heard people talking about what they were going to do when they were free of the place. Nick felt a deep sense of satisfaction knowing that he had made a difference in the lives of others.

Nick and G had become much closer. The two of them spent a lot of their time patrolling the shelter together. They talked about everything under the sun and found that they shared many things in common. G had also lost his wife due to complications that arose after she had received treatment for cervical cancer. Neither had any children and both of them had done their best to transition into the civilian sector before the collection had come and screwed everything up.

The mysterious observers of the shelter had been watching. The sense of community that had developed inside the hellish compound had gotten the attention of someone because the iron hatch opened once again. But this time a small contingent of reptilians entered the shelter each holding a rod that emitted a quivering blue light at the end. Not as many people scurried toward the shadows of the cell as they once had. Some even remained where they stood, proud and confident. The guards were quick to notice the changes in the behavior of their human captives. From among their ranks, a larger greenish reptilian stepped forward carrying a tablet. It was the same kind of device Nick had seen Dale use in the mine. With a flick of his wrist, the lizardman threw images upon the highest portion of the most visible wall of the cell. The images were three-dimensional busts of fifteen prisoners. Nick and G's faces were among them along with everyone who had assisted in the distribution of the MREs. The guard gestured for those he had identified to come forward. After everyone was accounted for, the prisoners were corralled into a single file line. The lizardmen then took their rods and held them up to the detainees' necks. The blue lights that flashed at the end of the rods flared outward forming bands of pulsating electric energy. The bands ensnared the prisoners around the neck. Nick was amazed at the level of technology he was seeing. He could also tell that if he were to try moving against the rod's snare it would prove to be painful. An awkward silence ensued as they were led out of the shelter one by one. Nick, being the last in line, couldn't help but look back upon the saddened eyes of those who were being left inside. The guard with the tablet slammed the hatch shut and cranked the wheel into its locked position. The sounds of a hundred fists beating against the scalding hot door could be heard from the outside. Nick wanted to cry but instead turned around to face his future and what he saw blew his mind.

Nick's jaw dropped as his eyes fell upon a massive underground city sprawling outward beyond his vision. The shelter he had endured was but one of hundreds, possibly thousands. The group of prisoners was marched down a wide gangway overlooking a cavity that housed level after level of identical prison compounds. Nick could feel all the prisoners crying out even though he could not hear or see them. The subterranean complex was lit by heavily saturated red lights, so hot they might as well have been heat lamps. Their powerful glow made it seem as though they were trapped in a sinking submarine. Reptilians of all sizes skulked about busily completing unknown errands. The guards brought the humans into a series of open-faced stalls with complex-looking notches cut into their walls. With the detainees still attached, each of the guards locked the ends of their rods into the notches, then left the area altogether. Once the reptilians had gone, Nick tried talking to G, but a sharp electrical charge tore into his esophagus. He got the hint and kept his mouth shut. He just stood there looking at the wall in front of him for what seemed like hours. Every so often one of them would be taken away but there was no telling where or by whom.

After quite some time had passed a woman's toned arm suddenly grabbed at the restraint rod in front of Nick. She jerked it violently from its place and pushed Nick ahead of her. Together, they exited the stall and negotiated a winding system of corridors. As they ventured deeper into the macabre maze the lights changed taking on a more clinical, hospital feel. The two of them ended up in an examination room of sorts where Nick was ordered to sit on a padded chair which automatically tightened on his limbs with an impersonal hostility. The woman, who sported a blond crew cut and a very muscular frame, wore a sleeveless white and grey unitard. It was a peculiar outfit designed to look futuristic and athletic. The woman locked the rod which held Nick's neck into another fixture on the wall behind him. She then started performing a series of medical examinations. After she was done probing his body with a myriad of devices, she broke into Nick's liquid bandages using a tool that looked very much like something a dentist might use to remove tartar from teeth. It was a painful process but once the hardened liquid bandage had been suctioned from Nick's wounds she cleaned them thoroughly by pouring iodine onto them. Nick clenched his teeth while cursing under his breath at the woman's heavy-handed method of providing aid. Once his wounds had been disinfected, she stitched them up after applying a local anesthetic. When she was finished the woman grabbed Nick's neck restraint and forced him into an adjacent room where his head was shaved by a machine. His body was sprayed down with cold water and soap, like a car wash, then deloused. Afterward, he was led into yet another smaller room. The woman pressed something into the middle of Nick's back and spoke to him firmly.

"Do you feel that?" she asked. Nick nodded his head. "This is an orbital plasma cutter. I am going to release you from your neck restraint. If you try to run, or if you try to assault me, I will put a hole, the size of a quarter, straight through your body. When I disengage your restraint you will enter the next room and put on the outfit on that bench. Do you understand?" The woman's words were as cold as ice. It was clear she meant business.

"I got it," Nick answered, knowing the woman wasn't his enemy. He wasn't about to make a break for it, not yet. Escaping into the underground complex at this point would've been pointless. Even if he did manage to kill a couple of lizard guards he would have no idea how to return to the surface. For all he knew they could be a mile or more underneath the surface of the earth. The woman retracted the electrical band from Nick's neck and pushed him in the back with the plasma weapon.

"Go!" she ordered.

Nick stepped into the next room which was conspicuously the same size as a lift. A pocket door quickly slid closed and separated him from the blond-haired woman who observed Nick with unflinching blue eyes through a small rectangular window in the door. Nick looked down at the bench sticking out from the wall. Resting on it sat a folded green unitard similar to the one the woman had been wearing. He wasted no time putting it on and was surprised at how well it fit. The unitard was made of a reflective, breathable material that covered Nick's entire body including his feet. He turned to face the woman and waited for further instructions, but she said nothing. Instead, she pushed a button on her side of the door and a new set of doors closed blocking Nick's view of the woman entirely. The entire room began to rapidly descend until it came to a jarring halt. Nick felt heavy, deep rumblings coming from outside. The room he was in trembled and, when the doors finally opened, Nick was let out into a packed arena. The cheers of grunting, howling reptilians hit his ears like a battering ram. All around him, sitting in tiered sections overlooking the arena floor, were thousands of lizardmen peering down at him. Nick glanced back at the elevator but it had disappeared. A huge monitor, the kind you would see at a sports venue, displayed a rotating image of Nick's visage along with glyphs that must have been written in the reptilian's language.

The arena's floor was made of decomposed granite. Nick knew what it was because he had used the tough earthen mixture in the backyard of his now burned-down house. Asymmetrical metal ramparts of different sizes and shapes rose from the ground like the haggard teeth of a giant dragon. The ex-soldier walked forward into the focal point of a spotlight shining brightly from above. From behind the furthest rampart on the opposite side of the arena appeared another man wearing a light blue unitard. They both looked at each other in confusion not understanding what was happening. That's when a reptilian voice, speaking English, called for silence. It took several moments but the whole place quieted down significantly.

"Only one of you will make it to the surface. Only one of you will survive. Kill your opponent and gain your rightful place in the new world. If you refuse to fight you will both die," the reptilian voice rasped. *"Begin!"*

The man wearing light blue was shaking horribly. He was not built for such a violent confrontation. Nick, however, had been trained by the strongest military force in the world to survive these types of encounters, but that didn't make it any easier for him to carry out the cruel command. The ex-soldier was troubled. Killing a person, who didn't know how to fight, was against everything Nick stood for. He had come to a crossroads. He couldn't engage. It simply wasn't in him.

"I can't do it." He told the man in blue who looked back at him with the same earnest sentiment.

"This shit is crazy, man! Look, I don't even know if my family is alive right now. I don't even know if I want to live, let alone fight." The man poured his heart out. A look of sheer desperation spread across his face as he stood there dumbfounded at the level of disregard for human life shown to them.

"You have ten seconds to engage. If you fail to act you will both be gassed to death," the gnarled voice from the PA stated.

Nick was fed up. The shelters were one thing, but the arena, the idea of killing regular American citizens, was diabolical. He didn't know what to do. Nick used the ten seconds to rack his brain for a solution. Only one came to mind and it was the craziest thing he could've ever come up with. Nick figured, he had already killed one reptilian. Why not try for another? And if he failed, he would die knowing that he had chosen the only fate that would allow him to keep his dignity.

"No, I don't think so! I won't fight another human for your sake. But I will fight one of you rat bastards! You hear me? Why don't one of you cowards come down here and fight the two of us? And if we win we both go free!" Nick challenged the lizardmen at the top of his lungs.

"What!? Are you out of your goddamn mind? What the hell are you doing?" the man in blue pleaded as he began to pee himself. Nick could see his unitard dampen around the groin. "That's a horrible idea, man! I'd rather be gassed than have to fight one of those things. C'mon!"

"Look, keep your shit together and we both might just survive," Nick told the man out of the corner of his mouth. "What's your name?"

"K-Kevin. Kevin J-Johnson," the man in blue stuttered.

"Okay, Kevin. Now, I've killed one of these things already. They *can* die--" Nick wasn't allowed to finish his sentence. The voice from the PA broke in accepting the challenge.

"*Challenge accepted.*" The voice then addressed the reptilians in the stands. The whole place erupted in a terrible fervor. Nick couldn't even hear himself think. The lizardmen banged their clawed fists against any flat surface they could find causing the whole place to tremble as if an earthquake were shaking the arena. Nick looked over at Kevin who was almost in tears at the thought of having to face such a fearsome opponent. Hundreds of reptilians volunteered to participate in what would most likely be a one-sided bloodbath. But, from among them, one was chosen. From four stories up a large creature with blue and red markings jumped down to the arena floor and landed on all fours. The reptilians chanted the creature's name over and over again, 'Brol, Brol, Brol, Brol!' It bared its jagged teeth to instill the fear of hell into his human adversaries.

"Oh, shit, man! Shit, we're gonna die! We're gonna die!" Kevin couldn't stomach his fright and, without letting Nick give him any pointers, ran off toward the portion of the wall that had once housed the same elevator from which he had emerged. It was a big mistake. Nick knew Kevin was as good as dead but his vulnerability would give Nick crucial seconds to devise a method for surviving. Sure enough, the creature went for the weaker man first. Several ramparts blocked Nick's view of Kevin's demise but he could hear the poor man's screams along with the sounds of his flesh being ripped apart. Nick was about to run over to a vent to try and pry off its metal grating when time seemingly stood still. Nick gasped at the incomprehensible nature of his situation. There was no sound or smell. The entire world had just… stopped. Nick began to walk around the frozen spectacle of mayhem when a voice, as calm as the surface of a lake spoke, to him. *"Do not be afraid. You will not die today. Rip the creature's tongue from its mouth with all of your might. Do this and you will be spared."*

The voice quieted just as quickly as it had appeared. In an instant, the scene around him came alive again as though someone had pressed 'play' on a VCR. Nick didn't have time to question what had just happened. The lizardman had finished slaughtering Kevin Johnson and had turned his unblinking yellow eyes toward Nick. The creature stood on his hind legs to present itself, all seven feet of him. With human flesh dangling from its pointed teeth the predator began to stalk its prey. The mob of lizard people went wild with the anticipation of more bloodshed. Nick had been told what to do by someone or something. It didn't matter who or what it was. He would take whatever help he could get. The only thing left for him to do was execute.

A powerful spirit of conviction fired within the ex-soldier which gave him an unreasonable amount of confidence. He moved without thinking and ran toward a rampart keeping it in between him and the lizard. The reptilian jumped ten feet into the air from a dead stance alighting onto the object Nick was using as cover. It swiped at him from above scraping the side of the battlement with its mighty claws. Nick ran to yet another smaller fortification in hopes of dodging the monster's next attack but the lizardman cunningly predicted his strategy. The reptilian jumped, not onto the rampart, but toward the wall facing it. He then repelled himself directly at Nick who saw in that exact moment his opportunity to carry out the mysterious voice's instruction. He stuck his arm straight out and into the lizard's opened mouth as it lunged toward him. The creature clamped down on Nick's arm and shook it furiously. It was like being attacked by a shark. Nick, using every bit of strength he could summon, fought through the pain and managed to get a hold of the lizard's slippery, muscular tongue. He jumped into the air and placed his right foot on one of the faceted edges of the rampart and the other against the creature's own body and pulled with all his might. The lizard reeled in response and fell on its back in hopes that the sudden momentum would force Nick off and away. It was the wrong move. As the lizardman's body tipped backward Nick sent his right arm even deeper into the creature's mouth, shredding his flesh on the beast's sharp teeth. Nick twisted around toward the top of the reptilian's head. The creature clawed at him viciously, but the ex-soldier couldn't be shaken. It was all or nothing for Nick and he knew it. He placed his feet against the reptilian's broad shoulders and gave another powerful tug. Nick could feel the ligaments that held the creature's tongue in place separating from its jawbone. Bloody gurgles came from the lizardman's open mouth. The serpent tried in vain to free itself by rolling over on its belly, but the pain the creature was experiencing was too great and prevented it from achieving its desires. Nick, abandoning all fear, thrust his other hand into the beast's mouth and yanked its tongue clean from inside it. When he brought the bloody tongue up and over the lizard's face Nick could see that the ligaments that connected the tongue had also been attached to the back of the reptilian's eye sockets as well as to the base of its brain. Severing it had killed the lizardman instantly. But the cost had been great. Nick looked at his right arm and threw up whatever was inside his stomach. His bloody limb had been gnawed to the bone. Streams of blood spurted from his exposed arteries. Nick was overcome with both unbridled joy and all-consuming nausea. If only Tommy could have been there to witness his victory.

Nick quietly staggered to the center of the arena and with his better arm held up the severed tongue, dripping with blood, toward a stunned audience. The lizards were silent. They couldn't believe what had just occurred. It was clear, even in Nick's battered state, that what had just happened was unprecedented. Breaking the silence, the reptilians began pouring the greenish-brown sludge they had been drinking onto the dirt floor of the arena in an apparent sign of respect. Nick was dizzy and sloppily issued a war cry. The loss of so much blood had drained him. He passed out still holding onto the reptilian's tongue along with a large portion of his honor, the lion's share.

CHAPTER SEVEN

Birthright

Brandon awoke in a dark, dusty chamber. An electric lantern placed by his head glowed softly and lit up a small portion of his surroundings. Brandon rose to his feet and took in a deep breath of chalky, putrid air. After a quick investigation, the young man realized he was in an ancient Chinese tomb. No doubt he had been brought there by the same people who had airlifted him and Speer off of the remote island. The young man picked up the lantern and began to search for an exit or any means of escape but the only door to the tomb had been sealed shut. There were no other sizeable openings of any kind. There had to be a way out, his life depended on it. The musty tomb had a finite amount of oxygen and there was no real way for him to know for certain how long he would be able to survive inside it.

As he gently ran his fingers over the shallow glyphs carved into a nearby sarcophagus, Brandon realized exactly where he was. He wasn't just in any burial chamber.

He was in the royal mausoleum of the dynastic families in Shaanxi. Brandon's mother had taken him to the very same tomb when he was just a small child. She had told him that their distant ancestors had once been great rulers and that their expectant spirits would be watching over him. In those days it had been a popular tourist attraction which is why he didn't immediately recognize it. Gone were the barriers keeping people away from the precious artifacts and the didactic panels had been removed as well. Brandon seemed to recall something in the news about the tomb having been built unknowingly on top of a major fault line.

Brandon's attention returned to the names of the dead carved into the sides of the stone coffins. He began looking for his own ancestors. Reading the classical Chinese characters proved to be a real challenge. Luckily, Brandon's grandfather had taught him the characters that signified the members of their royal lineage. Sure enough, deep inside the heart of the chamber, he found six sarcophagi bearing his family's ancestral name. That's when he saw it. He had almost missed it entirely. One of the coffins was much newer in appearance than the others. It looked as though it might have been placed in the tomb only recently. There were no cobwebs or dust on any of its surfaces. Brandon raised the lantern toward the inscription on the coffin. What he saw made his heart beat wildly. He couldn't believe what he was seeing. There, carved in rich detail, was his name. He wondered if he would have been buried inside it if he had lost the fight against the reptilian. After a brief moment of reflection, Brandon tried sliding the lid open. It was extremely heavy and barely budged when he strained to move it. He needed something that he could use to pry the lid open. Brandon went on the hunt to search for such an object. Lying in a narrow drainage ditch that ran along the mausoleum floor was an old section of security railing partially covered in loose dirt. The young man couldn't believe his luck and picked up the long piece of iron before returning to the coffin that bore his name. After exerting a great deal of energy, Brandon managed to muscle the lid off. The heavy stone slab crashed to the floor, breaking into two giant pieces. Brandon looked inside but there was nothing, only a gaping black hole. He hurriedly rigged the lantern to the end of the metal railing and lowered the light into the emptiness of the sarcophagus. He was shocked to find a narrow staircase leading into the darkness. Brandon smiled awkwardly. He was confident that he had found what was most likely the only means of escaping the crypt. He cursed his father under his breath as he lowered his Oxfords onto the cramped stairwell. It was a long descent down a narrow stone staircase. Brandon was accompanied by his memory of the Dutchman. Their epic kiss played over and over in his head causing him to wonder if he would ever see Speer again. He put his emotions aside for the moment as he came to the end of the stairwell. Brandon found himself in a secret catacomb filled with elegant horseshoe arches sitting atop fluted columns. The archways lined up with one's line of sight to give the impression that the room had infinite proportions. Brandon wandered through the seemingly endless interior until he happened upon a clearing. In the middle of the clearing light from a lone torch, held by a tall man accompanied by two others, danced against the all-consuming blackness of the catacomb. The three figures remained solemnly still as if in a trance. As Brandon got closer he saw a large red mandala-like symbol painted on the floor at their feet. He stepped into the torchlight and realized that the largest of them, the one holding the torch, was a lizardman shrouded in a black cloak. There was a much shorter man beside the reptilian who also wore a hood. The hooded man stood motionless next to a repulsive creature seated on a squat Roman-era curule. The seated being wore an ornate ceremonial garb that draped awkwardly around its emaciated limbs. Brandon stood on top of the arcane symbol and took in the most bizarre scene he had ever witnessed.

"Brandon Tsang," said the man standing next to the small throne in a muffled yet audible voice. He was wearing some type of black mesh around his face that prevented anyone from being able to see his face.

“Remain silent as you kneel before the vicar of our dark lord.”

Brandon knelt. He wasn’t sure why he complied so easily but he knew that he shouldn’t try anything stupid. The young man valued his life. Whatever he was being forced into, he just wanted it to be over. He wanted to go home.

The being in the chair sluggishly lifted its gnarled, shaking claw toward Brandon and said in a voice that could strip the bark off a tree, “You have been chosen, step forward!”

Brandon approached the grotesque being. The intense heat given off by the loud, crackling torch held above their heads was unrelenting. Without so much as a warning the thin, gangly creature sprung from its chair and threw itself at Brandon. The being bit into Brandon’s neck, crunching down onto the young man’s jugular. Brandon’s eyelids fluttered and he began convulsing uncontrollably. His vision went red and he could feel the hands of several men dragging him to the ground. He was tied down on top of the painted symbol and stripped naked. Brandon tried to scream for help but no sound left his mouth. Loud, ominous carnival music filled his ears and when his blurred vision began to return to normal he saw that he was the center of what seemed to be some terrifying ritual. Brandon panicked as he remembered what Alvarez had told him about the Order. A hooded figure came and stood above his naked body. The man was handed a red-hot branding iron which was made to look like a concentric maze shaped into the letter 'O'. The man didn't move but waited for another figure in a cloak to arrive holding a strip of what looked like tape. The tape was pressed down on top of Brandon's pubic region and violently ripped off carrying with it most of his pubic hair. Brandon screamed out as his body arched up off the ground. The hooded man standing over him then slammed the searing iron brand against the soft flesh of Brandon's pelvis pushing him flat onto the earthen floor. His skin sizzled and gave off the stench of charred skin. The man removed the brand and inspected his handiwork before angrily tossing the glowing brand to the side. Finally, a ladle of alcohol was poured out over Brandon's wound. The young man's body arched upward again in agony and stretched his bonds taut. The hooded man, still straddling Brandon, pulled out a white rag, doused with Chloroform, and put it over Brandon's nose and mouth. Brandon's eyes closed and his body went limp.

The lizardman holding the torch passed it to the human standing next to him. He then circled the throne and swiped at Brandon's restraints with his powerful claws. The reptilian picked Brandon off the ground effortlessly and turned to face the seated being who gestured for the young man's body to be taken away. The lizardman knelt and bowed his head in acknowledgment before skulking off into the shadows of the catacombs.

∞

Brandon regained consciousness. His vision was a little blurry but he was sure that he was back in the presidential suite of the Royal Meridian. He was dressed, head to toe, in a suit of fine quality similar to the one that he had been wearing at the onset of his fated trip to the island. It was nighttime and everything around him appeared just as it had been when he agreed to accept Olivier's gift. Had he dreamt the entire experience? No, Brandon knew better. He felt an itching in his groin where the brand had been seared into his skin and there was gauze taped over the teeth marks on his neck. "Welcome back, Brandon. I trust you had quite the eye-opening adventure, did you not?" Olivier asked, refilling two glasses of whiskey that were resting on the glass coffee table. He handed one of them to Brandon's father who was sitting across from his son staring at the young man angrily. Charlie took the drink from Olivier without breaking his gaze.

"What the hell is going on? What have you done to me?" Brandon screeched, scoffing at the notion that he was supposed to simply carry on as though nothing had happened to him. Seeing his father eyeing him kindled a spirit of intense rage in Brandon. He began to hear a salacious fog of whispers rising through the firmament of his mind. The voices urged him to strike his father down right where he sat. They accused Charlie and insinuated that he alone was to blame for everything that had happened to his son and that Brandon would not know peace until the dishonorable man was dead. Brandon had never experienced such forceful internal dialogue and was altogether confused as to where it was coming from. He thought that maybe a new, more confounding trick was being played on him. Brandon was snapped out of his train of thought by Olivier's even-keeled voice.

"What you have experienced in the last seventy-two hours was real, Brandon. But I promise you that the worst is behind you. You excelled at the challenges placed in front of you and have been found worthy of your father's legacy. Congratulations, young man."

"My father's legacy?" Brandon mocked. "What about all the men who were slaughtered by that - - that thing?" Brandon's shouting alerted the armed men who clicked the safeties off on their weapons just in case. Olivier gestured for his men to stand down yet he remained unapologetically silent.

"Those men died with honor in the heat of an ancient ritual between man and beast. Do not mourn their deaths. I know all of this must be difficult for you to absorb but you really must try and relax," Olivier suggested. The Belgian's eyes were cold and dense. It was clear to Brandon that the Belgian was devoid of empathy. "Let the events of the last few days melt into your memory. You are now one of us, Brandon, lock, stock, and barrel. Well, let me be honest. You are not one of us. You are far better than us. You see, the Order, whom I serve unquestioningly, has gone to immeasurable lengths to procure your membership. You are the future, Brandon, and we have made it a priority to seek out only the best, the brightest, and the bravest to lead humanity into a new age - the Age of the Order."

"I'm the future? If that's true then why is my father looking at me as though he wished I were dead?" Brandon asked with tears in his eyes. He tried looking at Charlie but his father turned his head in disgust.

"Because I do! How could you dishonor me, your family? Everyone saw you kiss that man! Everyone!" Charlie shot to his feet. He was livid, yelling at the top of his lungs. "No son of mine would ever kiss another man! No wonder you are slow to find a wife. You're too busy sleeping with other men!"

Charlie's harsh words gave Brandon every justification to surrender to the voices that demanded the man's death. Brandon looked upon his father's shortcomings as though they were tattooed on his forehead: adulterer, gambler, rapist, drunk, drug addict, pervert, and swindler. Everything that was wrong with society was embodied in his father's lecherous nature. Brandon, goaded by the forces of hate swelling within him, decided right then to cleanse the world of the foul man's presence.

"No, father! It is I who wish you were dead! You are the scum of the earth. I refuse to feel ashamed for whoever or whatever you think I am!"

"You should have died in that cave! I would have been so happy seeing that monster feed on your bones. I don't want you! Nobody wants you except your whore of a mother!" Charlie revealed his true intentions in the heat of the moment. The admission was the justification Brandon had been looking for. Alvarez had been right. Charlie had wanted to sacrifice Brandon for the sake of his wealth and position within the Order. His survival had been unexpected yet he saw that Olivier, unlike his father, had been pleased by his safe return.

Brandon picked up the brass dragon ashtray from the side table next to Olivier and hurled it at his father's head. It connected with such ferocity that the force of the blow knocked Charlie into one of the armed guards who kneed the older man in his stomach for getting too close to him. Charlie slumped to the ground bleeding and began crawling pathetically toward the entrance of the suite. Olivier sat back and watched the confrontation with keen interest while quietly sipping his whiskey.

"How many years have I watched you cheat on my mother with diseased hookers? How many times have I heard about your perverse desires? No, no more!" Brandon intercepted his father's feeble escape and smashed him in the face twice with his rock-hard fists. Charlie's face looked as though he had been hit with a sledgehammer.

"Don't do this! W-what about your mother?" Charlie mumbled, his swollen mouth full of blood and broken teeth.

A firestorm exploded in Brandon. His face turned beet red as he strangled his father to death. Without the slightest hesitation, Brandon picked Charlie up off the marble floor by his jaw and dragged him up the short private staircase that led to the roof. Spurred on by mysterious spirits Brandon threw Charlie's body off of the top floor of the Royal Meridian. As soon as he let Charlie's body drop the heaviness inside Brandon turned into bliss. His lifelong victimization at the hands of his father was over. Brandon didn't even bother to watch Charlie crash through the sunroof of a stretched limousine parked in front of the lobby on the ground floor. The soft, supple voices in his head that pushed him over the edge and into a maelstrom of evil quietly praised the young man. He was convinced of the necessity of his actions. Baptized in death, free from all responsibility, Brandon walked back inside and asked Olivier for the bottle of Yamazaki.

Olivier remained seated and watched Brandon swig down half the bottle of Japanese whiskey like it was bottled water. "Don't worry about Charlie, Brandon. The Chinese government decided to halt his beloved bank's expansion into the western provinces and there are rumors that there would be no more new branches allowed anywhere on the mainland. So, it's natural for a man under such extreme pressure to commit suicide. Especially on the eve of handing the family's financial empire over to his son whom he just found out was a homosexual."

Brandon stopped drinking and looked at Olivier without blinking. He knew the cover story would stick even at the cost of his fledgling reputation. He imagined reading it in the papers in the following days. His thoughts turned to his mother who would be both pleased and heartbroken by the news of her husband's death. Pleased that her cheating spouse had died, but heartbroken that he had committed suicide, which would make others think that their family hadn't made the man happy in life. Such a stigma would make it harder for Brandon's sisters to find husbands. Brandon accepted that the Order was real and that he was now one of them. He also knew that Olivier had most likely wanted Charlie dead, otherwise he could've easily stopped it.

"So, what are the rules?" Brandon asked, hoping to make more of an impression than his father.

Oliver smiled and went to ash his cigar but the tray was still on the ground covered in Charlie's blood. He waved for one of his guards to bring it to him. Without cleaning it off, the guard placed the bloody brass dragon on the coffee table. Olivier took a long and flavorful drag while fixing his coal black eyes on Brandon and answering, "There are no rules, Brandon. There is only the *will* of the Order."

CHAPTER EIGHT

Red Moses

Leila's relationship with her new friends had deepened significantly. It was as though she had three parents and two homes. If she wasn't helping Angela garden, cook, or clean then she was learning Wing Chun at the dance studio in town. Leila had become one of Darius's star pupils and had even impressed Xavier so much that he began to teach the little girl how to do all sorts of cool engineering feats. He showed her how to hotwire an old car, solder circuits, and use handguns. Days turned into weeks and the young girl's life was abundant with joy and hard work. Leila was slowly but surely rediscovering her effusive personality.

"Did you add the turmeric, Leila?" Angela asked coming in from the garden with a basketful of freshly picked alfalfa.

“Yup, and I stirred it for one minute. The beef tips are simmering and I already chopped the onions and diced the garlic.”

“Very good. You can put the garlic and onion in with the meat now. I’ve washed these vegetables. Would you please slice them into thin little pieces like I showed you?”

“Okay,” Leila replied, happy to carry out her share of the kitchen duties. She was so grateful to be living with Angela and the feelings were mutual.

The two of them spent another hour preparing their supper before sitting down in the living room to eat. They dined on seasoned beef tips served on a bed of couscous and alfalfa. The food was delicious. After dinner, Angela opened a bottle of locally-made fruit wine and shared it with Leila, who had taken a shine to getting drunk. They told each other jokes and played cards just like Leila used to do with her mother. Angela put some African music on her toy record player. Its joyous sound filled the tiny cottage with mirth and they danced until it was almost time for bed.

“Where did you get that mask?” Leila asked, pointing to where the strange object hung on the wall.

“You mean that one made of ash?” Angela replied.

"Yeah. It's so different from the other ones."

"A farmer from the Congo gave it to me in exchange for a ride into town many years ago."

"What do you know about it?"

"It is supposed to protect this house from evil spirits. It is a Chitahuri."

"A *Cheetahoori*? What's that?"

"In Africa, we have many legends about lizard people. My uncle used to tell me how the Chitahuri used to rule over all the world a very long time ago. They were cruel and mischievous. He told me that if I ever saw one I should be very careful because the Chitahuri are devilish and cannot be trusted."

"Have you ever seen one?"

"I have not. Do not worry, my child. It is only a legend."

"They must be very scary looking," Leila added not wanting to reveal the truth of their existence to Angela, even though she felt obliged to tell her. She still didn't think anyone would believe her if she talked about what had really happened to her.

"Yes, but I do not believe in them," Angela said, then paused for a moment. "The mask used to scare me. Look at it: it's very frightening. For many years I kept it in the shed. But one night, a robber came to my door and Shima ran him off. So I put the mask on the wall to scare people away just as the farmer, who gave it to me, told me to do."

"And do you feel safe now?"

"Yes, but I try not to look at it." Angela and Leila laughed changing the topic of discussion. "Let me tell you another story. It is the story of creation as it was told to me by my grandmother. Would you like to hear it?"

"Okay! Is it like the Bible?" Leila chirped in excitement as she plopped down on the couch.

"I will let you decide. I am afraid I do not know much about the Christian God," Angela answered and cleared her throat. She got up from a cushion on the floor and turned the lights off in the house. After going outside to shut the noisy generator off, she came back in and lit several candles to create the right mood for storytelling. Leila loved the way the shadows from the masks danced to the rhythm of the candles' flickering flames.

Angela took a seat next to Leila on the couch and began. "Long ago, before anything had been made, there was an endless ocean of blackness. Inside this great black ocean, there was no life. There was no light. The darkness was alone and knew only itself, but it longed to be happy. So, it decided to make a drum out of its own skin. It beat the drum with as much strength as it could hoping that something - anything - would come to dance and give it some company. The darkness kept the drumming up for a long time yet nothing came to dance to the music. The darkness cried because it thought it was the only thing anywhere. Yet as it cried, bits of it fell away from itself and became the twinkling stars. The darkness was happy to have company and began to play its drum like: '*dik-da diky dik-da diky*'. The stars, hearing the nice rhythm of the darkness, began to dance to the music. Not wanting the stars to leave, the darkness drummed harder and stronger than ever until it began to sweat. The sweat fell onto the drum which was very hot because of all the drumming and a giant star was born. That star was the Sun. The sun began to sing to the music from the drum which made the darkness very happy. But the darkness became tired and it asked the sun to drum for it a little while so it could rest. The Sun gladly took the drum and began to play a good steady beat like this: '*ka-boom tik ka-boom ya ka-boom ya ka-boom tik*'. After the darkness had rested it wanted the Sun to give the drum back but the Sun wouldn't listen. It couldn't hear the darkness over the sound of the singing, drumming, and dancing. This made the darkness very angry. It wanted to play and make the Sun sing and the stars dance but it could not. So the darkness angrily split the Sun into two pieces. It made one of the pieces the Moon. And it told the Moon, *'Because I have made you, you must always listen to me. You must never sing or drum. But when I tell you, you must ask the Sun to give me back my drum so I can play. The Sun will listen to you because you have a strong voice and it can understand your language.'* The Moon agreed to do what the darkness had asked because it was grateful to be alive. In a short time, the heavens played the most beautiful music you could ever imagine while the moon listened quietly and everything was good. But the darkness grew weary of the same songs the Sun and the stars would always sing when it was asleep. The darkness dreamed of building new instruments to play but there was no wood, goat hide, or sinew. All it could make was a drum, the same old drum. The darkness thought for a long time about how to make new instruments. So, the next time the Sun gave the Moon the drum to give to the darkness, the darkness told the Moon to keep them for a while. The darkness wanted the Moon to play a different tune while it slept. The Moon was so happy to play its music that it wept tears of joy. The Moon played a wonderful rhythm that sounded like '*da-kook kook bay dee, da-kook kook bay dee badam badam bay dee*'. Soon, the Moon's tears piled up until they formed vast oceans that stretched out as far as the eye could see. But the darkness became jealous of the Moon's wonderful sound and took back the instruments it had given the Moon, which made the Moon very sad. The Moon then cried tears of sorrow which also fell into the sea. But this time the Moon's tears were very heavy and made of dirt. Over time mountains formed followed by valleys and trees. And from within the lands, many different types of animals came to life. Seeing what the Moon had done, the darkness was happy again because it had found what it needed to make new instruments. It made a trumpet from the ram's horn and the kimbangala from the goat's belly. The darkness made many new instruments and, to repay the Moon for its good work, gave all the instruments to it saying, "take these instruments while I sleep. I have decided to let you play them for me. But you must play a different song every night." The Moon agreed and it began to play so sweetly that the darkness never woke. The Moon knew that it should stop playing so that the darkness could rise and take the drum from the Sun. But the Moon loved to play and didn't want to be silent and alone. So it kept playing afraid that the darkness would take away its instruments. The Sun and the stars loved to hear the Moon's songs. And so they agreed to divide the earth in half. That way the Sun and the Moon could play music all the time. But if the Moon ever stops playing, the darkness will wake up and become very angry that it has been asleep for so long. And we will never know when that will happen, but it could be tomorrow, or, maybe, the day after that."

Leila clapped her hands in delight. "I love that story, I've never heard it before. I love how the Moon was sad and then became a trickster but only because it loved music so much!"

"Yes. I often think about this story and what it means. I do not think I understand it, but I am sure that my grandmother did."

"What do you think it means?" the little girl asked.

"I don't know, Leila. It is just a story. But when I was a little younger than you I used to think about it a lot. I would take guava from my grandmother's yard and sit under a rubber tree. I would be very quiet and try to listen out for the sound of the Sun's drum." Angela paused while reminiscing about her childhood. Tears started to well up in her eyes as her memory conjured up a world of emotions. "The Moon knew how beautiful music was and when the darkness took it away it cried tears of sorrow. That is why all living things are a little sad because we are born from sorrow. We all remember the beauty of music even when darkness takes it away from us."

Leila began to cry, too. She understood what Angela had said. Every living thing had a memory just like when she touched Ruby and saw its life play out in her mind's eye. Angela's explanation of the story was the most beautiful thing the little girl had ever heard. How else could you put something so profound into words that even a child could understand? She hugged Angela with the utmost compassion and, as she touched her, Leila saw the sequences of the woman's entire life flow across her mind. She saw Angela, alone, working tirelessly against the arid earth as a child. She then saw Angela's mother's death and all the events that led to making Angela the kind and generous woman she had become. And most importantly, she saw herself within Angela's spiritual journey and knew immediately that she meant a great deal to her.

Leila walked outside to get some fresh air and gather her thoughts. She stared up at the moon and thanked it for its honesty, for its longing. And she saw within its beige brilliance the sadness that she now knew all too well. She cried again, silently, sitting down on the porch of Angela's small clapboard cottage and contemplated her life. Leila didn't quite comprehend the timing of her ability to view someone's past but she did grasp its relevance.

Inspired by Angela's childhood, Leila clambered up the steep hill behind the cottage. She went straight for the mango tree and plucked the ripest mango she could find. Leila rested her back against the trunk of the mango tree and peeled the red and green fruit revealing its sweet golden meat. As she enjoyed her sticky treat she looked off into the distance toward Tutu Town, which was aglow, but something was wrong. The glow was much too bright to be coming from the lights of the villagers' houses. She soon realized, after noticing tall plumes of greyish-black smoke rising into the night sky that the village was on fire. Leila threw the barely eaten mango to the ground and limped back down to the cottage as fast as she could without falling over. Angela wasn't in the living room or the kitchen. She had gone to bed early without cleaning up the kitchen, which wasn't like her at all. Leila pushed open her bedroom door without knocking only to find Angela crying by herself. Leila ran up to her and gave her the biggest hug she could.

"What's wrong? Why are you crying?" Leila asked.

"I am fine, Leila, thank you. I miss my mother. She has been dead for so many years but I still feel her spirit inside me. When I told you the story of the Moon and the Sun I was reminded of her."

"You must come up to the mango trees with me and see. Tutu Town is on fire!" Leila said as she stood at the door ready to run to the backdoor.

"What? Are you sure?"

"Yeah, come and see. Hurry!" Leila urged. The two of them ran back up to the top of the hill. Angela gasped at what must have been a desperate situation for so many of her friends who lived in the heart of the town.

"Come. We must go and see what is happening. This is not good. We'll take my moto."

They walked as fast as they could to Angela's shed. She prepared the gasoline and oil mixture, but, as they were starting the motor, Xavier's orange Land Rover roared up the driveway. Darius was driving it alone. He had a panicked look on his face and honked the horn several times to make sure he got their attention.

"Leila! Angela! Get in the truck. Hurry!" Darius ordered from inside the cab. "There are men with guns coming this way. Hurry!"

Leila and Angela didn't ask any questions. They both trusted Darius. If he said danger was on its way it meant that their lives were truly at risk. They locked the shed and jumped into the Land Rover. When they got to the main road Darius engaged the four-wheel drive and passed over the road and straight into the bush. The thwacks and scrapings of the chaparral against the truck's metal exterior heightened the drama of the moment.

"What is happening? Who is responsible for this?" Angela asked.

"We don't know. Five trucks, some with armed men, pulled into town an hour ago and started rounding people up. They tied up their hands and feet and threw them into the back of the trucks. A handful of villagers used whatever weapons they had to fight back but there was little they could do. When the trucks drove off the men inside them set fire to the village. We have to get back to Xavier. He was trying to prevent the militia from destroying the power plant when I left to go and get the both of you. The marauders are gone but they were last seen heading down the road toward your house. There! Look! You can see for yourself."

Leila looked out of the window to her left. Off in the distance, small bursts of bright orange could be seen roiling against the dark greens and greys of the night. Angela cried out as she got a good look at all the fires. Troubling images of her neighbor's suffering filled her mind with agony.

"They must be going from house to house!" Angela noted in shock. "Who are these men? Where do they come from?"

"The chieftains think they are Congolese. They are not from Mozambique. I couldn't make out their dialect."

"They could be General Watodja's men," Angela stated in disgust.

"Yes, but if they *were* Watodja's men they would have taken our provisions," Darius added.

"Who is Watodja?" Leila asked, as their truck hammered its way through the chaparral toward the village.

"He is a warlord from Zambia, a very corrupt man," Angela replied bitterly.

Darius pulled into the outer edges of the burning city. He drove at a snail's pace so that they could take their time assessing the damage. They passed by the smoldering ruins of the open-air market. The vendors' wares had long been removed but the infrastructure for their pop-up shops lay in ashes along with many of the permanent roadside shops. Fortunately, the fires were being put out just as the flames began to climb up toward the villagers' homes that had been built above the stalls. Hundreds of people ran to and fro trying their best to tame the blaze. Others carried the injured to the small white hospital that served as a rallying point for everyone in Tutu Town.

"Darius! Please, let me out here!" Angela pleaded. Darius stopped the truck and let Angela get out. "I will help Dr. Mebina at the hospital. Leila can go with you."

"Fine. We'll meet up with you later, Angela," Darius said.

"Please be careful, Angela," begged Leila, waving goodbye to the large woman as she exited the truck.

Darius drove on until he reached the small power station at the north end of the village. By the looks of it, only one of the generators had been damaged. Sparks shot off the small field of pylons that flanked the main control room and the bodies of several dead men lay scattered about. Darius parked the Land Rover underneath a makeshift carport next to the control room's entrance.

"Come with me, Leila. Stay close!" Darius and Leila got out of the truck and began searching the power plant for any sign of Xavier. They finally found the engineer and several other men from Tutu Town in the heart of the control room. They were standing around a young man who was strapped to a green desk chair. Leila could tell that Xavier and the others were trying to interrogate the man by beating him with the metal tools they still gripped in their hands. Leila was horrified. She was appalled at Xavier for having participated in such a violent act.

"Stop!" she yelled at Xavier and his accomplices, "Leave him alone! You're going to kill him!" The older men looked at one another in bewilderment. They had never been spoken to like that by such a young girl.

"Dammit, Darius, why did you bring her in here?" Xavier asked pointing his bloodied wrench at Leila.

"Because I happen to agree with her, mate. You need to stop this right now. If he hasn't told you what he knows, it means that he's more frightened by whoever sent him than he is of you."

Leila approached the young African whose face was covered in burn marks and fresh, tender bruises. He could only see out of one eye. Xavier attempted to stand in the girl's way but she shouted at him. Xavier immediately stepped back and lifted his hands surrendering to Leila's will. She eyed the other men who could only shake their heads in confusion.

Leila stepped directly in front of the young man in the chair. She leaned in closely and whispered a question into his ear, "What's your name?"

"Peter," the man uttered through swollen lips. Xavier raised his eyebrows in shock. They had been trying to get the guy to talk for almost twenty minutes. And just like that, the man opened up to Leila in a matter of seconds. Darius gave Xavier a look of astonishment. Both were curious to see what other information she could pry from their prisoner.

"I'm sorry they did this to you. It isn't right," she apologized softly, "but they're just trying to protect everyone who lives here. Why do you want to hurt us?"

"Construction in the north. They need more workers. They sent us to get as many people as we could fit into the trucks," Peter answered in hushed tones, his black, quivering eyes just inches away from Leila's. She remembered that the Setian guard from the shelters had warned Leila not to venture north but it still wasn't clear why. The young man knew he had already said too much. He lowered his head and refused to answer any more of Leila's questions. Xavier stepped forward readying his pistol for a kill shot, but Leila intervened. She begged him for just one more minute with Peter.

"If he doesn't talk, he dies, Leila! His men caused untold amounts of damage tonight. He must pay for what he has done," Xavier commanded while looking back to the men at his side who nodded their heads in agreement.

"Wait a moment, please," Leila requested. Xavier reluctantly backed off again. Leila took a deep breath and then placed her tiny hands around the young man's head. Just as it was with Angela and Ruby, Peter's entire life leading up to that very moment streamed into Leila's mind. She could see that, as a child, Peter had been regularly beaten by one of his uncles. She could also see that, after bludgeoning a friend to death over the affections of a girl, Peter had spent years running from the authorities. But it is what Leila saw next that truly troubled her. She saw the man Peter worked for. He had on large black sunglasses, wore a red bandana over his face, and carried a large gold-plated assault rifle slung over his shoulder. Peter's memory showed the man doing business with the Setians in a land to the north. Peter and his comrades were providing them with laborers in exchange for food, weapons, and petrol. The young man had told the truth. The reptilians were sending war parties into the surrounding regions to fill their labor quotas. Leila removed her hands from Peter's head. She lifted his chin and whispered one final question into his ear.

"Who is the man in red?"

Peter looked up at Leila with eyes as big as saucers. He didn't understand how she could have possibly known about his leader. Fearing the little girl's mysterious abilities, he quietly answered her. "Red Moses. He is Congolese, like me. He always drives the biggest truck. He wears a red hat. Always something red."

Leila turned to address Xavier, Darius, and the two other men who had been effectively sidelined. She, again, decided to leave the Setians out of her description of what was going on. She knew that if she talked about the lizard people they wouldn't accept any of the information she needed to pass on to them.

"The leader is called Red Moses. They need people to work in the north. That's where they're taking everybody."

"Thank you, Leila. I have no idea how you got him to talk but it doesn't matter now. I will discuss the matter with the men behind me. They are chieftains of the village," Xavier said as he holstered his sidearm. Leila bowed her head awkwardly at the chieftains who eyed her warily in return. "Darius, everything is fine here. You and Leila should go now. I will get a ride home with the chiefs." Xavier threw a knowing look at Darius who reached for Leila's hand in acknowledgment.

Before they left Leila walked up to Xavier and pulled on his shirttail to get his attention. "Please, Xavier, don't kill Peter. He's just a boy. Promise me you won't kill him?"

Xavier looked at the young man in the chair pitifully putting his hands on his hips. He sighed and then looked back down at Leila. "Okay."

"Promise?"

"I promise not to kill him."

Leila hugged Xavier and then returned to Darius's side. They walked out of the control room together, hand in hand. When Xavier and the chieftains were out of sight

Darius picked the young girl up in his arms and started kissing her all over the cheeks and neck. She giggled but then looked Darius firmly in the eyes. "Everything's gonna be different now. Red Moses will come back."

"You're right, Leila," Darius agreed as they walked out to the car. "I will take you back to the hospital. You can help Angela and Dr. Mebina. I'm going to check on the studio. So, are you going to tell me how exactly you were able to do all that back there?"

"I can see into people's past. Not everyone's, but some people. I don't know how it works exactly. But if I care about someone, and I touch them, then I can see their lives in my head," Leila said, jumping into the passenger seat of the Land Rover.

"Have you seen my life?"

"No, it doesn't work like that." Leila laughed, "I can only do it when someone needs me to, almost like an emergency or something."

Darius dropped Leila off at the tiny hospital which was still humming with activity. She, along with Angela and a host of other volunteers, worked well into the night on behalf of Dr. Mebina. They applied salve on burns and did their best to remedy the effects of smoke inhalation for all who needed it. There were at least a hundred people who needed medical attention at the hospital but thankfully no one had died. There were not enough cots to go around and most everyone had to lie on the ground in and outside of the small white building.

"Leila, Dr. Mebina wants me to go with some men to the houses along the road. We have to see if the people who live there are okay. Do you want to come or would you like to stay here?" Angela asked.

"I want to go with you," Leila answered, sharing a look of grave concern with Angela. The two of them got into one of three vans heading that way. They stopped at the first turnoff that intersected with the main road. They assessed the damage to the farmhouses there before hopping out of the van and helping all those who had been burned and injured. To their dismay, the people who lived outside of the village center got it much worse than the villagers who lived in town. Red Moses's men had shot and killed everyone's livestock. A few people had died trying to protect themselves and their property but almost everyone else had been abducted by Red Moses's men. Only the elderly were left behind.

Leila and Angela helped load the vehicles with a few who were injured along with the dead livestock. They were all taken back to Tutu Town, the animals to be processed by the butcher and the people to be delivered to Dr. Mebina. Instead of waiting for the caravan to return to drive them to the next grouping of houses the two friends decided to walk.

The warm night air hung low and heavy. The sliver of a moon did little to light their path. As they journeyed farther down the unpaved country road Leila told Angela about what had happened with Peter at the power plant. Leila could see that her words deeply worried the woman who walked most of the way in silence, just listening.

"Tonight, many people who have never spoken to each other opened their hearts. Many have heard rumors of these work camps. But the people were too afraid to talk about them."

"Why?"

"I don't know. Africans can be very superstitious. Sometimes, if you don't talk about something it goes away. And sometimes when you talk about something too much it turns into reality."

"Do you think the villagers will fight back?"

"No, I don't think so. Our village is just a small trading town. There are very few men of fighting age here."

"It's so sad. I like it here. Do you think everyone will move away?"

“I suppose so. I am thinking of going to my sister’s village on the coast. I have been told it is much safer. They say there are many young fishermen there who can help protect the village.”

She and Angela turned right down the next road just as one of the vans returned. The driver stopped and the two friends got inside. They drove toward the next group of properties that had been pillaged by Red Moses. Leila didn’t want to leave the bustling little town that she had begun to call home. Where would she go and who with? There was no telling what the future would bring for Tutu Town. Leila read the writing on the wall and knew that she would most likely be leaving the village soon. How she longed for the stability of her family and their home. And even though she tried to suppress the memory of her mother and father, she began to see their smiling faces in everyone she came across that night. Leila didn’t know if she would ever see them again. She cried to herself as she accepted the bitter reality that she probably never would.

CHAPTER NINE

The Eldred Queen

Nick opened his eyes. His eyelids burned and felt as heavy as stones but he was grateful to be alive. He had somehow survived yet another encounter with a lizardman. Nick looked around the room he was in. It was nothing more than a large metal box with a bed, desk, and chair. He felt like a dump truck had driven over him. He lifted his right arm and rested it against his forehead as he did so often after waking. Nick quickly shot up when he realized his arm had been miraculously restored. He could move every finger on his right hand just as nimbly as before he had thrust them into the gaping mouth of a fanged reptilian. The skin on his new arm was a lighter complexion than the rest of his body and he felt almost nothing when he touched it. Nick had no idea how long he had been unconscious, but it had to have been long enough to heal from major reconstructive surgery.

Beyond the foot of his bed stood a metal door with no handle. Nick approached it cautiously not wanting to burn himself in case it, too, was scalding hot. He tested it remembering to use his left hand. He was relieved to find it cool to the touch. Nick pushed the door open but it didn't budge nor did it automatically open in response to his presence. His movements did, however, prompt a projected image to appear on the blank wall catty corner to the door. The image was of a large grey letter 'C' with an 'O' inside it designed to look like a maze of concentric circles. Underneath the logo in a minimal, futuristic font were the words 'Omnus Corporation'. Nick had never heard of such a company. Underneath the logo was an italicized slogan that read, *"A new world for a better humanity"*. A blue button at the bottom of the screen blinked to indicate that it was to be interacted with. Nick touched it not thinking anything would happen but the projection did respond. A loading page sprang up. It took some time to connect to whatever it was searching for but, after a few moments, an older man's face appeared. He had short, well-groomed greying hair and coal black eyes. Nick could tell it was a live feed and that the man was observing Nick with great curiosity.

"Nicholas Camby! I see you're feeling better," the man said in a cordial voice. "How is the new arm working out for you?"

"Fine, thanks," Nick replied in a loud voice brimming with conviction. "You mind telling me just what the hell is going on around here? I have rights dammit! I am a United States citizen and I demand to be released!"

"Nicholas, I understand you are confused, and rightfully so, but before we begin this conversation you must agree to be civil. Failure to pass this most basic psychological examination will result in your readmission into the shelters. Now, have I made myself perfectly clear?"

Nick was taken aback by the calm, pragmatic tone of the man's voice. The man couldn't have expressed the severity of the situation any better. Nick, not wanting to go back to the shelters, acquiesced.

"Okay. Okay. I'm listening."

"Good. My name is Dr. Robert Calahan. I am the Director of Matriculation for this facility. It is my job to ensure that all potential citizens of Omnus have been mentally, emotionally, and physically adjusted for orientation. Now, what I'm about to tell you will most likely cause you some emotional duress." Calahan said as if reading from a script he'd rehearsed thousands of times. "Reactions might include nausea, vomiting, anger, depression, rage, suicidal thoughts, guilt, shame, anxiety, discomfort, and or any combination of the aforementioned psychological conditions. I would also like to inform you that this conversation is being recorded for the sake of the Omnus Corporation's records. I must now ask you to state your name fully and whether or not I have your permission to proceed."

"My name is Nicholas Camby and, yes, you have my permission to tell me what the hell is going on," Nick answered sarcastically. The doctor sat back in his creaky office chair putting a little more distance between himself and the camera lens he was looking into. He sipped a cup of tea to clear his throat then began to speak.

"The world you once knew before the collection is gone, Nicholas. Every government institution, and every military organization from the old world has been dissolved. Their combined resources have been appropriated by a private entity called the Omnus Corporation, which I represent. The collection, in reality, has nothing to do with safeguarding the citizens of sovereign nations against the threat of deadly solar flares. It is, rather, a massive filtration project aimed at repopulating the earth's surface with people whom the Omnus Corporation deems fit to pass on their genetic material. As of this moment, 1900 hours on October 30th, you are officially being offered citizenship within the Omnus Corporation's network of cities for the following reasons: upon your entry into shelter 00252B2 on August 20th, 2036 at 1600 hours, you slowed the rate of its attrition by thirty-four point seven percent. On September 26th, at 1700 hours, you were removed from shelter 00252B2 and proved your physical superiority over a Kevin Johnson, of shelter 00237B1, and thus claimed your rights as a citizen of Omnus. Do you confirm or deny the occurrence of these events? Please answer."

"Confirm, even though I didn't kill him," Nick seethed. There wasn't even a trace of emotional off-gassing coming from Dr. Calahan's diatribe. It was airtight. The man must have given the same speech to countless others ahead of Nick.

"The lizardman you are referring to is, in fact, called a Setian. They are a highly intelligent terrestrial humanoid species that have been living on this planet since the Triassic Period. They, along with the Omnus Corporation, have reorganized the earth's resources, geography, and infrastructure. As an intended benefit of our mutual endeavor, large portions of the equatorial and subequatorial regions of the planet have been allocated to the Setian species for their recolonization. Omnus, on the other hand, has constructed nine 'megacities with the sole intention of housing fifteen percent of the total human population. The remaining human element within the shelters, including all humans who chose not to register, will become the property of the Setian Empire to be used or disused according to their own interests."

A long silent pause came next as Dr. Calahan waited to observe Nick's reaction to the most sinister yet matter-of-fact bomb anyone could ever drop on another human being. Nick was at a complete loss for words. He could only remember the most heinous bits about the attrition rates and people becoming the property of the reptilians, or Setians. He had no idea what to say or think. It was as though he were playing chess against the most advanced computer in the world. He had been checkmated at the outset of the conversation. The way the doctor presented the information allowed no room for doubt, curiosity, rage, or anything. Nick felt as though someone had just sucked all the air out of the room and his lungs.

"To conclude this interview with flying colors, Nicholas, you only have to say the following words. Failure to do so will result in your reintroduction into shelter 00252B2. "I, Nicholas Camby, being of sound mind and body, have received this information in good faith and hereby claim my rights as a citizen of Omnus."

Nick paused. He witnessed his value system get mowed down by the fear of being readmitted to the shelters. But they were just words and as he repeated them to Dr. Calahan's projected face he now knew he had no other choice but to escape or die trying. He would take no part in a new world order built on the death of America, a country he loved more than life itself.

Nick had grown up hearing about the atrocities the American government doled out to minorities across the board but the current situation was altogether different. How had the American government given up its power? How did a country like North Korea simply agree to end itself? Nothing made sense at all. The level of intricacy involved in dismantling such robust global powers was unimaginable and yet the Omnus Corporation, a completely unheard of company, had succeeded in doing just that.

"Congratulations, Nicholas Camby. You have been cleared for orientation. A representative of the Omnus Corporation will collect you in exactly twelve hours to escort you through the facility. It will be quite confusing your first time out. Your door will remain locked until after your first day of orientation. After that, you may come and go as you please. Oh, and I must warn you that the Setian you managed to kill inside the arena has made you somewhat of a celebrity around here. I suggest you prepare yourself. Show your fellow citizens a modicum of respect and an appreciation for your shared hardships. Good night, Nicholas. Try to get some sleep. You have a big day ahead of you tomorrow. Welcome to Omnus."

A host of powerful emotions flooded through Nick. From that very moment, the Omnus Corporation gained his ultimate respect as well as his undivided hatred. He could only assume countless others were going through the same process at the same time. The projection cut off and the cool greyish-blue tones of the smooth metal wall took its place. Nick let out a scream that shook him to the core but was successfully stifled by the acoustics of his tiny room. He beat his fists against the wall where the projection had been swearing up a storm until he was spent. Nick wouldn't be a part of any of it. He had to get out. It was all bullshit. Everything Dr. Calahan had told him had been scripted. There was no doubt that the reason for its concise delivery had been deception. He had to think. He wasn't going back to the shelters alive and he sure as hell wasn't going to become a part of any new world order. He had to find a way to get back to the surface and warn Tommy and the others. If he did manage to escape he would have to fight his way out against human and Setian guards alike. Nick tasked himself with the impossible mission and sat down on his bed with his back straight. He would have to wait for the precise moment to act and when it presented itself he would have to be ready.

The digital alarm clock affixed to the wall close to Nick's bed sounded off. It read 0800 hours. He had been lying still for the last six hours cultivating the readiness and fortitude needed to escape. Nick knew that if ever there were a chance for him to leave the underground complex now was the time. He took deep breaths in and out as he waited for his escort. It wasn't long before Nick heard an impatient rapping coming from the other side of the door to his room. Nick sat up but didn't answer right away. He rounded his shoulders slightly and smoothed out his right angles. He didn't want to appear anxious or angry.

"Who is it?" Nick asked.

"I am here to escort you to the first phase of your orientation. Are you ready?" a man replied in a British accent. There was a slight tinge of irritation in his voice.

"Come on in."

The metal portal slid open and a stiff, slim man with curly auburn hair and sharp green eyes stood in the doorway. He returned Nick's gaze, apparently unimpressed with what he saw.

"Nicholas Camby, I presume?" the man asked.

"Yup, and you are?"

"Balthus Hatton. So, you're the one who slayed the great beast? I don't suppose you'll want to be called Saint Nicholas from now on?"

"No, I don't think so," Nick replied unaffected by Hatton's dig. The guy obviously had a beef with him. Nick couldn't care less. He knew that if he was to escape, he would have to choose his battles wisely from here on out.

“Let’s go. You shouldn’t be late for your first appointment. Please, follow me.” Balthus turned and started walking briskly down the corridor that led away from Nick’s quarters. He kept a good pace and Nick had to trot awkwardly behind him to keep up. The section of the underground complex they were in was much different from the shelters or the arenas in that it appeared to be designed for comfort and relaxation, not intimidation and control. The lighting and the contours of the structures they passed were the product of thinkers and artists, not spartan military engineers. As they walked through the complex Nick looked for any means of escape: ventilation ducts, emergency doors, stairwells, and maintenance shafts. Soon, the two men came to an elevator. Hatton called the elevator and a few seconds later it showed up. They entered inside and as soon as the doors closed Nick tried his hand at sparking up a conversation to gather as much intel as he could.

“How far down are we exactly?” Nick asked.

“I don’t know. I haven’t been told. I can tell you, however, that we will be going up to subdeck seventeen.”

“Did you have to fight in the arenas?” Nick questioned, trying to peel off a few layers of the man’s lackluster personality.

“Yes, everyone has to fight,” Balthus responded, his eyes remaining forward staring at his blurred reflection in the stainless steel elevator doors. There were no buttons inside only a black security scanner with a sleek numeric punch pad.

“Yet, you’re still here, underground. Why? Shouldn’t you have moved on by now?”

“I asked to work for Omnus to elevate my citizenship status. They are the new masters of the world now. It would serve you well to fall in line or else you just might not ever see the sun shine upon that scarred face of yours again,” Balthus warned.

Nick said nothing more. Balthus wasn’t the kind of person Nick wanted to associate himself with anyway. The elevator finally came to a stop. Upon exiting they walked past a series of well-lit labs protected by thick panels of soundproof glass. Nick could barely make out people in full body scrubs dipping materials into narrow stainless steel vats with colored gases issuing from them. There were armed guards everywhere, some standing watch and others patrolling the floor in pairs. Balthus came to a door opposite the labs and waved his hand in front of another black scanner that was housed inside the door jamb. The door spoke requesting the entrant’s name. Balthus provided his name clearly and pointedly.

It opened and Balthus gestured for Nick to continue on by himself.

"When you are done here have the staff notify me. I will return to take you to the lecture hall at approximately 1100 hours." Balthus didn't wait for Nick to repeat his instructions. He just turned on his heels and rid himself of his charge. Nick shook his head, thankful to be free of Balthus's company. If Nick had been placed into the arena with the likes of Hatton he never would have fought the Setian. But for whatever reason, the universe decided to pit him against a peaceful do-gooder.

Nick stepped into an empty blue-tiled room. He took it upon himself to sit down on one of the chairs that lined the wall closest to the exit. The room was filled with half-made gadgets and tech whose functions were impossible to figure out by just looking at them. It was kind of a mess inside. High up in the corner of the room hung a large flat screen that played a slideshow of images depicting a series of futuristic cities full of strange architecture and sweeping vistas. They were probably Omnus cities, Nick thought. Nick looked around for anything resembling a weapon but found only small electronic parts and exceptionally thin screwdrivers. He thought of his best friend again. Tommy could have most likely made a neutron bomb out of all the stuff in the room.

“Good morning!” exclaimed a disheveled middle-aged man with chin-length mousey brown hair. He was wearing thick glasses and a lab coat that looked two sizes too big. “Nicholas Camby? Hello, my name is Dr. Istle, and let me tell you what an honor it is to meet you.” The doctor held out his hand and shook Nick’s vigorously. Istle’s introduction was a welcome contrast to Balthus’s cold disposition.

“The pleasure is mine, Dr. Istle,” Nick replied, smiling. He instantly liked the doctor who appeared to be honest and intelligent.

“Everyone saw you kill that Setian in the arena. The way you pulled out its tongue like that, wow. That was amazing! Who knew you could kill one that way? I’m still learning so much about their biology. Did you know they can see in the dark... like cats?”

“How were you able to watch my fight?”

“They televise them, of course,” he said as he searched through the mess in his lab for the tools he would need. “You wanna know something else? All the fights are pre-recorded before they’re broadcast. Omnus had to stop showing the fights live because so many people are refusing to fight each other. So, they edit those matches out and only playback the nasty ones.”

“I don’t understand. Who watches them?” Nick wanted to know. The evil of the Omnus Corporation seemed to have no end. Nick was somewhat relieved at knowing that his reaction to the arenas was more typical than he had thought.

“Everyone in the megacities of course. You can learn a lot about people by observing how they respond to violence. I understand the fights are hard to stomach, but they are, nevertheless, quite instructional. Please have a seat over here and roll up both sleeves for me,” Istle said, running off to an adjacent room separated by a large floor-to-ceiling window. The doctor returned, carrying a laptop with him, and took a seat next to Nick. Istle took out three pieces of chewing gum and popped them all into his mouth as he synced up the device to his laptop. “Would you like a piece?”

“No thanks. Wait, I don’t follow. You’re telling me that people are living in those cities already?” Nick asked pointing to the monitor in the corner of the room.

“Of course. Why wouldn’t there be?”

“So, they never had to go into the shelters or the arenas?”

“Nope. Oh, that’s right. You don’t know. I forgot. They told me you never registered. If you had, you would have been given the option to buy your way into one of the Omnus cities. The people that could afford it went straight there. Everyone else was collected."

The bad news just seemed to keep coming. While billions of good people all over the world had been thrown into the most vicious proving grounds imaginable, the super-rich had just waltzed right into a veritable utopia. Nick thought back to the motto written underneath the Omnus Corporation's logo, '*A new world for a better humanity*.' What a crock, Nick thought. The whole notion of paid citizenship was abhorrent to the ex-soldier who was taught to believe that money couldn't determine the worth of a citizen. Nick suddenly eyed Istle's happy-go-lucky attitude with suspicion if not contempt.

Nick sat down and held out his right arm. Istle analyzed it with great interest. He was using a tool that looked like a jeweler's loop and as he passed it over Nick's limb it relayed high-resolution images to Dr. Istle's laptop. "Ha, your arm is some of my finest work, Nicholas. I know this will sound kinda weird but I am glad to be a part of you. Here, take a look."

Istle handed Nick his laptop. The doctor moved the viewing device over his skin. Nick could see every vein, artery, and muscle in real time. He made a fist and saw his blood vessels inflate while the muscles contracted. Then, he relaxed his hand and watched his blood vessels deflate as his arteries swelled with oxygen-spent blood.

"So, you're the one who brought my arm back to life, huh?" Nick said, feeling such a sordid mix of emotions it was hard for him to be grateful. Nevertheless, he was impressed with Istle's abilities as well as the examination device he was using.

"It took me two weeks to graft new replacement tissue for you. I took skin from your buttocks, outer thigh, and muscle fibers from your right quadricep. Then I spliced them together with stem cells and a new synthetic hormone called DH-28. I grew you a new arm directly on top of the raw bone that was still in place. The stem cells carried out their instruction perfectly. In about a month you should recover all of the feeling in your right arm. Because of your injury, I'm going to have to place your STAR chip in your left hand for now. Once you have completely healed, a doctor on the surface will reinsert your data chip into your right hand where it belongs. We like to use the right hand because it is furthest from the heart."

"STAR Chip?"

"Yes, it's an acronym. Subdermal Tracking and Reconnaissance. It's your basic subdermal data miner/transponder. Over time it will meld with your body's tissue thereby making it impossible to remove without surgery. Consider it an internal prosthetic. Every citizen of Omnus cities gets one." Dr. Istle held up his right hand to show Nick his own. The ex-soldier could see a little scar in between the doctor's thumb and forefinger. "The chips are a security measure that will allow the Omnus computer network to form a symbiotic relationship with your real-time biological data, social patterns, and consumer behaviors."

"So much for more privacy." Nick felt blindsided. There was no way he would be able to escape with a damn tracking device in his body. He felt the window of opportunity closing in on him. But something inside him told him to be patient.

"Not exactly. The network will know where you are at all times but not because it is specifically targeting you. There are no video cameras within the public spheres of the new cities. Omnus has been very clear about wanting its citizens to feel free and safe. And with Omnus' new satellite/drone relay system they can target microscopic objects at the drop of a hat without having to continuously monitor everyone. Not the Big Brother you were hoping for, huh? Haha. Now, I'm going to need your left hand if you don't mind."

Nick stuck his left hand out. Istle swabbed the webbing in between Nick's thumb and forefinger with an alcohol-laced cotton ball. He then made a small incision within Nick's skin. The doctor brought up a tool that looked like a glorified tattoo machine and shot a chip, the size of a grain of rice, into Nick's hand. Istle squeezed a bit of liquid bandage, the same kind Nick had used in the shelters, on top of the incision and waited for it to dry.

"Okay, great! Now I need you to go over there and place your hand in that black box for me," Istle instructed, pointing to the far side of the room. Nick did as he was asked. On his way there he got a chance to peek into the adjoining room. His heart just about jumped out of his chest at what he saw. Hanging on the torso of a mannequin was the very same thermo-optic camo Nick had seen the soldiers from inside the mine wearing. It was a veritable godsend. He couldn't suppress the smile spreading across his face. He had found the means he needed to escape and it was sitting just yards away. Nick cataloged its location and turned back toward the task at hand not wanting to spark suspicion. He focused on the small LCD monitor over the box that displayed his height, weight, age, sex, name, and birthplace along with a host of other medical designations most of which he couldn't understand.

"Now, Mr. Camby, we afford everyone the opportunity to change their name as a means of promoting a positive disassociation with their past. You may now choose a new name if you wish, a fresh start. I suggest doing this now as reprogramming a STAR chip, once it's been activated, is rather time consuming and requires a great deal of administrative support. Not to mention it leaves a ghost identity lingering in the system which then must be digitally isolated, quarantined, yadda yadda yadda."

Nick thought about it. "I'll stick with my given name. It's the only thing my mother ever gave me and I'm not sure I want to forget about my past."

"No problem. Please look over your information and note that I am erasing your previous known addresses, as they no longer apply."

"Everything seems fine," Nick stated. He was looking at many of the thin screwdrivers that littered the work tables in the room with an all new level of respect. He could use one of them to dig the newly implanted chip out of his hand. It might be painful but it would work.

"Alright. Just let me input my access code, scan my hand, and… BAM!" Istle shouted as he entered the final keystroke that programmed Nick's STAR chip. "Awesome, but we've got to test it, too. If you could kindly sit back down we can wrap this all up."

Dr. Istle scanned Nick's left hand and a three-dimensional image of the ex-soldier's face popped up on Istle's scanner along with all the relevant personal information. "Okay! It's official. Congratulations, Nicholas Camby, you are now a full-fledged citizen of Omnus. Whichever city you choose will be lucky to have you."

“Thanks,” Nick blushed. “Hey, Istle, I’ve got a question for you.”

“Shoot!”

“When I was collected, the soldiers that took me into custody were wearing some kind of optical camouflage. I’ve never seen anything like it before. They were somehow able to blend in perfectly with their surroundings. Do you know anything about that kind of tech? I’d really like to know about it.”

A grin that stretched from ear to ear spread across the doctor’s face. “Oh, yeah? Wait just one minute. Hehe.” Dr. Istle got up and ran into the other room but never returned. After five minutes Nick grew impatient. He walked over toward the room Istle had gone into but ran into something in the middle of the doorway. Nick reached out and felt for the invisible object. That’s when Dr. Istle pulled back the hood of the camouflage tunic he was wearing.

“Boo! Haha. Isn’t it incredible? No batteries needed!” Istle boomed. Nick pretended to be scared much to the doctor’s amusement. Istle then took off the tunic, ran over to a nearby table, and flipped the tunic inside out. “Fire-resistant thermal dampening mesh on the inside,“ Istle said, his eyes wide with excitement. Turning the tunic right side out, he continued, “micro-prismatic cladding on the outside. You can hide anywhere in plain sight and not be seen, or you can jump into the middle of a blazing inferno and not be cooked by the heat. Pretty cool, right? My team designed this more than ten years ago. The applications are endless. I'm just trying out some new things with this one."

"How long have you been working for Omnus?" Nick asked, preparing himself for the violent but necessary act he was about to unleash upon the unsuspecting scientist.

"Oh, for Omnus? Just two months. But I have been working on special research projects for the Department of Defense for twenty years," Istle stated, slightly distracted by a noisy mechanism malfunctioning off in the corner of his workshop.

Nick's intuition hadn't failed him. Every cell in his body fired simultaneously sending the same message to his brain: *Now*! Nick grabbed Istle, the only person in the lab, and choked him out ever so gently. The good doctor put up little to no resistance and was unconscious in seconds. Nick dragged Istle's body into a supply closet and hogtied him with a few extension cords he found lying around. He used Istle's tie to gag the scientist then softly closed the closet door and jammed the lock. Nick ran back to the table where the camouflage tunic lay and put it on before running into the other room. He found a small surgical scalpel amidst a tray of other tools and reopened the incision Istle had just made in his left hand. Nick then picked up a thin flathead screwdriver and after several seconds dug out the flashing green STAR chip from inside his hand. Nick dropped the chip to the ground and crushed it under his heel. He checked himself out in the large window pane that separated the two rooms of the lab. He couldn't see his reflection at all, even when he moved. Confident the tunic was doing its job, Nick hastily left the lab concealing the scalpel he had used behind his outstretched forefinger.

Dr. Istle would wake up soon. It was only a matter of time before someone freed him from the supply closet. Nick estimated he had about a fifteen minute head start. Heart pounding, Nick searched the floor for a way out. He might as well have been a ghost walking through the corridors as he cast no reflection, shadow, or heat signature. After touring the level, Nick concluded that the elevators, on either end of the floor, were his best means of escape. He opted for the larger of the two elevators thinking it would more than likely lead to less populated sections of the massive underground complex. He nervously waited for the doors to the freight elevator to open. He did his best to maintain his focus on what he would do once the freight elevator had arrived.

The metal doors of the freight elevator finally opened and several scientists wearing lab coats and ventilation masks exited carrying metal briefcases with warning labels plastered all over them. Nick stayed well out of their way and then slipped inside. He knew that freight elevators often had pressure sensors in their floors to calculate the weight of their cargo. So, he climbed along the lift's metal grating so as not to step on the sensors. He hung there until the elevator was called to another floor. Unfortunately, when the elevator did move again it went down instead of up. Nick cursed his luck and as the lift descended the temperature inside rose noticeably. Nick hung on the metal grating like a salamander on a wall as sweat dripped from his face. When the lift stopped again an enormous Setian entered accompanied by two human beings decked out in sleek yellow HazMat suits. The Setian was nine feet tall and there was no telling how much it weighed. The giant reptilian was olive green in color with massive shoulders and a thick muscular tail. It wore a leather codpiece, metallic greaves, and a blue cloak clasped at the neck. Nick took great care to slow his heart rate down hoping the occupants would disembark quickly. As the elevator rose upward Nick noticed the large Setian quietly sniffing the air. Unalarmed, the reptilian brought his head back down and continued looking over the information displayed on a digital tablet held in his giant clawed hands. The lift came to a stop and the two scientists exited but stopped when they realized the Setian wasn't following.

“Are you not coming, sir?” one of them asked the great beast in as polite a manner as possible.

“It seems I have forgotten something below. I will meet up with you shortly after I have retrieved it,” the Setian answered, speaking in a broad, booming voice.

“Okay, I guess we’ll begin preparing the specimens then. We’ll wait for you before we start the sequencing,” the other scientist added. The large Setian said nothing but simply nodded his head in approval.

The elevator doors closed again leaving Nick alone with the Setian. The ex-soldier began to panic. The creature was surely on to him. The reptilian typed in a passcode without scanning his hand and the elevator descended again even faster than it had previously. Nick was in trouble. He didn’t know what to do. Images of his fight in the arena played back in his mind. He couldn’t remember seeing a creature so large in the arena’s stands. It would be impossible to overcome him. But before Nick could calculate his next move the Setian spoke without looking directly at Nick.

“Your attempt at escaping this facility is as daring as it is useless, Nicholas Camby,” the Setian said confidently. “You may keep your camouflage on for the sake of the cameras but trust me when I tell you that your presence is as obvious to me as mine is to you.”

“How? How could you possib--,” Nick started to ask, but the Setian interrupted his question.

“Setians release a very distinct pheromone upon death. There are very few humans who smell of it, even fewer still who smell of two deaths.” The Setian paused, heightening the tension in the elevator that was already growing hotter and hotter the further down it went. “Tell me, Nicholas Camby, have you had your chip implanted yet?”

“Yeah, but I took it out.”

“Hmm. Interesting. And have you killed anyone during your attempted escape?” The Setian continued to look straight ahead. He gave the cameras no reason to suspect there was anyone else inside the freight elevator.

“No,” Nick answered, unsure if his honest response would have a positive effect on his chances for survival.

“Who was the last person you came in contact with?”

“Dr. Istle. I locked him in a supply closet in his lab.”

“Very well. You will do me the honor of accompanying me to Mu. There is someone I would like to introduce you to. It would be extremely unwise for you to refuse my offer.”

“Mu? What is that?”

“You will see soon enough. There are no pressure sensors in this elevator. You may step down if you wish. But let me warn you, when these elevator doors open you are to walk directly in front of me while remaining camouflaged. Failure to do so will put your life in dire jeopardy. Do you understand?”

“Yes,” Nick answered, hopping down onto the elevator’s floor. His fingertips were aching from having had to flex them around the grating. He had so many questions for the creature he didn’t know where to begin. He led with the most obvious one. “Why are you so much bigger than the others?”

“I am an Ok. We are the ruling Setian class. As in human society, Setians have a hierarchical social structure. But, unlike modern humans, we are a matriarchal culture.”

“Why haven’t you killed me yet?”

“I have my reasons. The most ardent being our shared disgust with the Omnus Corporation’s methods of operation.”

“I don’t get it. You’re helping them. How can you hate them?”

The freight elevator came to a stop and its doors opened. Intense waves of rippling heat invaded the lift taking Nick completely off guard. The Setian brought up his tablet and spoke into it using his native tongue. It sounded as though he was issuing commands to someone.

"Step forward and take heed to my warning," the Setian growled.

Nick walked forward and lifted his head. His eyes drank in the most amazing sight they had ever seen. The elevator had let them out onto the edges of an underground world so alien in appearance and design that Nick unwittingly stopped in his tracks.

"Welcome to Mu," the Setian stated as he pushed Nick forward. "Keep moving."

Nick looked out upon Mu as though he had just unearthed an ancient, lost civilization. He had been right the whole time. He knew it! There *was* an alien world beyond the door in the mine. Butterflies filled his stomach and each step forward gave Nick the impression that he was trailblazing a new frontier. Nick realized that he had been secretly waiting for a moment like this his entire life. The glorious discovery of a new world unfolded before him and caused his brain to flutter with ideas and concepts that, ordinarily, would have been completely out of the reach of his imagination. Nick gathered himself and did his best to put one foot in front of the other.

He walked on ahead of the Setian who made sure the human was walking in the right direction.

The architecture of Mu was a bewildering mixture of nature and industrial design. There were rows of buildings that looked very much like massive cobalt blue dominoes standing on end stretching out for miles. Other structures were interwoven into the natural rock formations of the vast cavern. There was light, but no sun. In its place hovered a churning ball of thermodynamic energy that lit the underground city with a bright orange glow. It gave Mu the appearance of being perpetually at dusk. Nick had no clue how all of this could have existed beneath the earth with no one the wiser. And if the government knew about Mu, which they most certainly did, how then had it been possible to keep such a secret?

The two made their way to a transport that resembled a snowmobile the size of a pick-up truck with tank treads. Nick climbed into the passenger seat and the Setian drove them through the inner workings of the city. Nick scanned every detail, committing it all to memory so that he could one day explain what he saw to Tommy. Their technology, like their architecture, was an indelible synthesis of nature and intention. Bioluminescent algae grew everywhere and emitted a soft fluorescent green light. The streets were made of solid rock but had been machined to create pleasing polygonal patterns of varying designs. Perfectly smooth sheets of water fell from slender openings within the rock walls that surrounded them and were used as media displays. Nick could tell by Mu's grand design that Setians preferred large, open spaces. They eventually drove into a section of the city littered with oddly shaped dwellings that resembled tall, narrow mounds. There were many different types of reptilians walking around. Nick saw old, young, female, and male Setians whose scales all bore different patterns and colorations. He marveled at how diverse their species was. He might as well have been walking through the streets of New York. There were scrawny Setians with bony ridges in the middle of their heads like mohawks and large brutish ones with menacing scowls and smooth bald heads. The females were far less colorful than the males, but much more visually appealing. They wore uniquely made clothing that could be loosely identified as being 'fashionable'. Nick was enjoying himself immensely until they got closer and closer to a silver spire that seemed to rise from the navel of the earth itself. The spire was well fortified by Setian guards numbering in the thousands. As they drove past the military formations the warriors became aware of the scent of death that Nick's sweat glands were emitting into the air. His presence, even though unseen, was fueling a growing discontent among the soldiers who eyed Nick's transport suspiciously. Nick experienced a new level of fear. Being surrounded by creatures so adept at killing made him wonder why the lot hadn't invaded the surface of the earth years ago.

The Setian stopped the conveyance when they came upon two formidable guards standing post in front of an immense metal door. They were both wearing brilliant ceremonial breastplates and greaves that appeared to have been made of a mixture of alloys and precious metals. Each of them held a sarissa tipped with menacing interlocking steel blades. Even though Nick could not be seen, both guards looked directly at him as though he were standing naked in front of them. Words and salutes were exchanged and, much like in a human military base, their transport was waved through. The giant door retracted in the most peculiar manner. It had been constructed with reinforced slats. Each slat, one by one, turned vertically on its axis, stacked themselves one atop the other, and then rolled upward along a track suspended inside the large tunnel the opened door had revealed. The Setian drove forward and then parked the transport at the tunnel's end.

"Get out and walk straight ahead. Do not stop for any reason," the Setian commanded. Nick did as he was told, passing through a long corridor that opened onto a wide bridge made of a beautiful translucent crystalline material. On the other side of the span, an elegant palace shaped like a slender teardrop arose. The bridge extended over an abysmal chasm that was so deep Nick could not see its bottom. As he crossed over it he observed the bridge's design and its structure with great curiosity. It was more of a walkway than a bridge. There were no barriers on either side which dramatically increased Nick's awareness of the bridge's height and also his complete vulnerability. It would be impossible for anyone afraid of heights to cross it. At any moment the Setian behind him could have thrown Nick off with but a nudge of his elbow. When they reached the other side, a retinue of guards, dressed in even more robust ceremonial armor, came to attention. They stood in formation on a shallow staircase whose width matched that of the palace. The Setian behind Nick roared something in his native tongue. The guards saluted in response by beating their chests and chanting something several times before instantly quieting like stone sentinels. The power of their sound-off gave Nick goosebumps. He sheepishly walked up the steps passing the awesome soldiers who remained perfectly still. He continued forward some hundred feet when he felt a giant claw rest on his shoulder.

"Stop here. Do not move." The Setian behind him meant to whisper. But even his whisper sounded like a guttural snarl. Beyond them were two massive iron doors four stories high. A musical instrument that sounded like a cross between a didgeridoo and a tuba bellowed loudly into the air. As its song subsided the colossal doors opened only slightly. "Walk forward, slowly."

They passed through the open threshold and into another colossal chamber that shimmered with transcendent golden light. Hand-beaten gold, silver, and platinum-hinged plates covered the interior of the palatial room. They refracted light emitted by giant hanging censers ablaze with crackling white flame. The slight clinking of the lustrous metallic plates against one another created a chime-like effect that was both soothing and ethereal. They continued walking toward five opulent thrones that sat proudly at the end of the chamber. Each throne was occupied by a creature as great in size as the one escorting Nick. Sitting on the central throne, the tallest and most ornate of them all, was a female Setian who seemed to be of great importance. She was wearing a long diaphanous gown that spilled down onto the pristine marble stairs beneath her. Her scaling was a pale pink and she wore a diadem made of the largest diamonds Nick had ever seen. The Setian walking with Nick stopped him at the landing of the stairs that ascended to the throne. A moment of silence passed between all who were present. The only sound that could be heard was the subtle clanging of the polished plates on the walls. One of the Setians to the right of the central throne spoke to Nick's captor in the reptilian's tongue, at length. The large Setian behind Nick responded in a voice that was both proud and respectful. The female sitting on the central throne smelled the air and took in Nick's scent, then looked eerily into the human's eyes.

"Remove your cloak, human. You are now in the presence of the Eldred Queen," the pinkish Setian said in a voice that resonated throughout the room. The ex-soldier could feel the powerful gaze of the Setian queen bearing down upon him. Without anyone telling him he knew that he was in front of the ultimate authority in Mu. She was not merely a figurehead like many of the leaders of human politics.

"After you take it off, kneel. And do not speak to or look directly at the queen," the Setian behind Nick rumbled. Nick removed his thermo-optic cape and folded it into his arm, then knelt down in front of the throne, all the while making sure to keep his head down.

"Achsocheles, why have you brought this human into our innermost sanctum?" the queen asked.

"It was by chance, my queen, that I discovered him trying to escape the matriculation. Considering his unique circumstances I took the risk of bringing him here so that you could examine him in person, Your Highness."

"It was prudent for you to do so, my son. I commend your ambition and continue to put my faith in your capable hands. You, unlike your treacherous brother, have proven yourself most valuable to the Setian throne."

"Thank you, mother," Achsocheles replied.

"What have you told this man about the Omnus Corporation?" she asked.

"Nothing, Your Majesty. I felt it not my place to inform him."

"Very well," the queen replied, and turned her attention from Achsocheles to Nick who remained kneeling. "Nicholas Camby, rumors of your exploits have traveled far enough to reach even my ears. It is not often that a mere man bests a Setian warrior in open combat."

"Why are you working for Omnus if you hate them so much?" Nick spoke out of turn. He then looked straight at the queen's blood red eyes much to the dismay of the royal retinue who twitched in their seats at the audacity of the human being in front of them. Achsocheles grabbed Nick by the throat and raised him into the air. As the Setian wrenched Nick's neck, the queen stopped her son by gracefully raising her hand.

"Achsocheles, this human being is not afraid of death. Threatening him with it is the sole reason why he has defected. Do not repeat the Order's mistake."

The mighty Setian dropped Nick to the ground without so much as a word. Nick knelt back down but repeated his question to the Setian Queen.

"Setians want nothing more than to reclaim our dominion upon the surface of the earth. Since the dawn of human civilization, we have conspired to control the political machinations of your species. But when the time came to initiate our great plan we were betrayed by the very people that provided us with the opportunity to recolonize."

"So what does any of this have to do with why you haven't killed me yet?" Nick held out his arms questioningly and looked at the queen for answers.

"You have seen the power that is responsible for bringing our world out of the darkness and into the light. We, Setians, call it the Eye of Ra. Much like nuclear power the Eye of Ra can be transformed into a weapon of incredible power. The digital blueprints for this superior technology are held within a device known as an oculus. This device has been stolen by one of my sons, Dyklotimus. The same power that we used to broker a deal with the Order is now threatening to divide the Setian Empire. Your duplicitous oligarchs have turned my very own flesh and blood against me! For this, they will pay, but first I need the oculus returned to me at once. Dyklotimus cannot be allowed to assemble a second

'Eye' -- which the Order will no doubt use as a means to rid the world of our kind. You, Nicholas Camby, are going to retrieve it for me."

"How exactly am I supposed to do that? This camouflage doesn't work around Setians. Your son, Dyklomaton or whatever his name is, will smell me coming a mile away."

"Yes, he will, but what he will smell will be me. When Dyklotimus fled with the oculus, he absconded with thirty of my bravest warriors who were once loyal to me and thus bear my scent. I will share my essence with you. And by using your cloak, coupled with the strength of my essence, you will pass undetected anywhere within the boundaries of the new city where he now hides like the coward that he is."

"New city? Where?" Nick asked.

"Dyklotimus has taken refuge under the aegis of my sworn enemy and sole rival to the throne, the Brood Queen. She is in the process of rebuilding our ancient capital, Avandar, in the heart of the Congo," the queen replied matter-of-factly.

"How many Setians are there? If your technology is as powerful as you say then why haven't you already taken control of the planet?"

"Our ancient empire, Lemuria, once ruled over all the lands but the Great Floods came and destroyed our beautiful cities. Those who survived hid inside the hollow earth far away from the salt waters of the ocean and the plummeting temperatures of the planet. And while your species flourished, using the knowledge we exposed you to, our kind licked our wounds in the darkness. To this day our numbers are too small for an open attack against humanity. And an all-out war would leave this planet, which is our ancestral home, uninhabitable. Setians have survived cataclysms before, but we will not be the cause of another one. If we fail to secure the oculus, I will have no choice but to use the Eye of Ra as a weapon. And as much as I don't want to, I will not hesitate to turn Avandar, and all those living within it, human or Setian, into a pile of smoldering ashes. "

Nick's mind began moving a mile a minute. Everything he had been taught in school had been but a shadow of the truth. And, as his mental landscape grew in its capacity to fathom the bigger picture, he realized he also had something else working for him that he never thought possible, leverage. He could barter the safety of Maranatha in exchange for accepting the Eldred Queen's mission. He had somehow found the power to save the lives of Tommy, Clarissa, Kai, and all the other Christians who lived in the camp. Nick was filled with the conviction of his desires and became convinced that, as unbelievable as it seemed, he had been consistently making the right decisions. It was as though he were being guided by some angelic spirit. The queen had been right. Nick wasn't afraid of death. He was afraid of losing his friends at Maranatha. And even though he wasn't a Christian, the tiny encampment became a symbol of human life and goodness, something Nick would die for even if he couldn't live among them.

"I will do whatever you ask of me but you must do something for me in return," Nick played his cards.

"Speak," commanded the queen.

"There is a small farming commune in the southwestern region of California near the border with Mexico. Leave that camp alone and grant me the necessary equipment to communicate with them on an ongoing basis. Do this for me and I will do whatever it is that you want me to do. I swear."

"Achsocheles, can this be done?" the queen asked. The large Setian stood up, took out his tablet, and began typing on its screen. Several moments later he responded to her.

"The region is well outside our interests, my queen," he answered dutifully.

“It is done, then. Provide the human with what he desires.”

“Yes, Your Majesty,” Achsocheles answered while bending the knee.

“Rise, human. I will share my essence with you so that all Setians know who you truly serve.” Nick struggled to his feet. His knees creaked slightly as he straightened himself. The eight-foot Setian queen unfolded her long gown revealing a long slit on its lower portion then descended the stairs that led down to where Nick stood. She held him fast with tremendous strength biting into his neck like a vampire. His body went rigid under the pressure of the queen’s jaws. He could feel and smell something pumping into his veins invading his body and mind. His eyes rolled back into his head and his body gradually went limp before he blacked out. The queen let the man fall into Achsocheles’s waiting arms. She spat the taste of human blood from her mouth and resumed her place on her throne. As the queen’s attendants wiped the blood from her jaws she watched Nick’s body as it was unceremoniously dragged out of the royal chamber.

CHAPTER TEN

Alpha One

Charlie Tsang's funeral was well attended by many of the major political and economic players from all over Southeast Asia. His wake was carried out according to traditional Chinese custom with a slight exception for the large numbers of paparazzi entrenched in the streets outside of the Huan Ming Temple. The media had swallowed the story Olivier had so callously outlined for Brandon: hook, line, and sinker. Brandon's mother, Vivian, didn't buy it at all. After years of being married to a man of such ill repute, she had developed a keen sense for foul play. She grilled Brandon daily asking him where he had been in the days leading up to his father's death. But his answers always remained the same. Olivier had instructed Brandon to tell his loved ones that he had taken a trip to a tropical island where he spent a few days relaxing on the beach. Anyone who had ever met Brandon knew that his love for sailing took him to many faraway, exotic places. Yet still, his mother kept pressing

Brandon for answers that he was unwilling to give. Perhaps, she felt guilty for not being a more accommodating wife. The fact that Charlie's life insurance policy paid out a whopping seventy-five percent of its total value surprised everyone in the family. The check, made out to Vivian Tsang, had been written out for ten million dollars. Brandon was sure the money was the motivation behind his mother's annoying inquisitiveness.

As Brandon held his mother's arm he did his best to be strong for her. He led her through the crowd of well-wishers and stopped at the large gold-framed portrait of Charlie. The enlarged photo had been airbrushed to eliminate the realities of aging. Brandon's two sisters trailed behind them sobbing uncontrollably. They held sticks of incense that they placed in front of the Buddhist altar in honor of all of their ancestors. While his mother and sisters prayed, Brandon's mind was clear of doubt, guilt, or remorse. He had watched Tsang Tao Bank's stocks plummet after Charlie's death, just as Olivier had predicted. Brandon shrewdly bought up as many shares as he could. When Brandon, heir to the estate, assumed the role of chairman of the board the news hit Wall Street with great verve. The price of the bank's shares skyrocketed and reached an unprecedented level. Brandon had made a whopping five hundred million dollars and secured an extra five percent of the company for himself, or rather his family. The nightmarish indoctrination into the Order had its perks. Everything he had been through now seemed like a distant memory.

The Tsangs rose to their feet and left the temple so that others in attendance would have the opportunity to honor Charlie's memory as well. Brandon's mother and sisters got into the stretched limousine that waited on them curbside. As Brandon followed them, a man from the crowd bumped into him and secretly placed a burner phone in the pocket of the young man's suit jacket. The stranger then walked off and disappeared among the crowd of photographers. The phone immediately rang and Brandon, surprised at the phone's sudden appearance, reached into his pocket and answered it.

"Who is this?" Brandon whispered into the phone knowingly. It could only be one person.

"Tell your family you will meet up with them in an hour. Tell them now." The voice on the other end was Olivier. Brandon could hear the Belgian's accent. He put his head in the limousine and explained to his mother that a few of father's ex-business partners needed a word. Vivian gave Brandon a hard time but finally gave in after he promised he would meet up with them at the restaurant where the funeral reception was being held.

"Okay. I am here but I don't have that much time," Brandon stated, as he watched the limousine carrying his beloved family pull away from the curb outside the temple. As soon as it had gone another fancier limousine pulled up in its place. The driver got out from behind the wheel and raced around to open the door for Brandon. Cigar smoke spilled out from inside. It was Olivier. Brandon got in and sat across from the man who wore an all-black suit with a single red rose pinned to his lapel.

"What's the occasion?" Brandon asked, smiling.

Olivier waited for the chauffeur to return to the driver's seat before answering. "I am the one who brought your father into our sacred brotherhood. It is customary for one who fosters such a relationship to show a modicum of respect. Quite frankly, Charlie was indispensable to the Order, that is, until you came of age."

"And how exactly was the Order able to benefit from my father's -- no -- my family's influence?" Brandon asked, cutting to the chase.

"That is no longer relevant. The reason I wanted to speak with you is that I made a promise to your father that I intend on keeping. I want you to take this…" Olivier said as he handed Brandon a small, innocuous USB drive. "When you are alone I want you to open its contents. Call me on the phone I gave you when you are finished absorbing everything on that drive. Do you understand, Brandon?"

Brandon held up and inspected the nondescript drive, "Yes, I understand."

"Good. You have twenty-four hours to call me. For the sake of your entire family I hope that you take everything I am telling you quite seriously," Olivier said while pushing a button on a panel next to his left arm. "Driver, pull over."

The stretched limousine pulled to the side of one of the busiest streets in the garment district. Without another word, the driver got out and opened the door for Brandon who exited the vehicle while keeping his eyes on Olivier the whole time. The unassuming Belgian seemed to have a firm authority wherever he went. Brandon took mental notes even though he did not aspire to live amid such secrecy as Olivier clearly did. The car pulled away from the curb and drove off, leaving Brandon alone on an empty sidewalk. There was still plenty of time to hail a cab. He just had to find one.

On the way to the reception, Brandon fingered the drive incessantly. He was beyond curious as to what secrets it would reveal. He had half a mind to skip the reception altogether just to find out but knew there would be hell to pay. The cab ride took a little under half an hour and when Brandon got out he was shocked to see so many mourners queued up for entry into the reception. The line practically wrapped around the block. Brandon strolled into the restaurant and took a seat next to his grieving family. They had no idea they were sitting next to Charlie's murderer. Even if someone had shown a video to Vivian Tsang documenting Brandon's culpability she would have said the video had been doctored. The Tsang family, what remained of it, was as loyal to one another as any crime family could be. The Tsangs spent the next few hours sharing anecdotes about the departed and getting drunk on *bai jiu (bye-joe)*. When it was time to leave, Brandon was secretly ecstatic. In a short while, the mystery of the flash drive would be over. The Tsang clan climbed into the plush limo and the driver, on the behest of Vivian, took the long, scenic route toward their oceanside villa, much to Brandon's dismay. Along the way she took the time to talk candidly to her children about the many positive things, Charlie had done for their family. She also detailed some of the legal issues of Charlie's will so that everyone, specifically her two daughters, would be better prepared for the weeks to come.

The driver parked the car in the driveway of the Tsang's beautiful three-floored detached home in Repulse Bay. Charlie and Vivian had moved their family to the quiet resort-style district when the youngest of the three children, Zi Yan, was born. Brandon was twelve at the time and spent most of his first summer at Repulse Bay sailing on the warm winds of the South China

Sea. The young man became quite adept at sailing. It had become an outlet that allowed Brandon to express himself without having to directly confront the issues of his own sexuality and his father's rejection. Regardless of the Tsang family's internal tensions, the children and their mother were in love with one another. Thankfully, for their sake, Charlie had spent most of his life away on business. When he returned, Charlie routinely found himself alien to the affairs of his household which, in turn, prompted him to stay away for longer periods of time. In the end, Charlie Tsang had done very well for his family by leaving them without debt or any bastard children looking for handouts.

"I am so tired," Zi Yan sighed, walking past her sparkling maroon Cadillac STS, the apple of her eye. "Mei Mei, watch a movie with me?"

"Okay, but only if Brandon brings us Haagen-Dazs," Mei Li, the second-born daughter of the Tsang family answered.

"Do this for your sisters, Brandon. And, please, when you are out, bring me noodles. I am starving. I couldn't eat very much at the reception," Vivian ordered.

"You're going to get fat," Brandon replied, not thrilled, but willing to complete the errands. The ladies protested by throwing their shawls at Brandon and punching him. Without changing out of his suit, the young man got on his Hayabusa and let the throttling engine convey his frustrations. His mother and sisters ran inside the house and closed the door on the horrible racket. Brandon sped off down the street and headed toward the town's center. Brandon had an aversion to driving cars. It was a claustrophobic experience for him. While sailing he had learned to enjoy the open air. Only a motorcycle could deliver both the exhilaration of speed and the freedom of movement he experienced while out on the water.

Brandon dipped and swerved through the backstreets of the town as he picked up the items for the princesses and the queen, as he so often called them. It took him more than an hour to complete the errands. Brandon was so excited to see the contents of the flash drive that he rocketed home as fast as he could and threw the bags of food at the foot of his front door. He then rang the doorbell and rode off toward the marina where his beloved ketch, the *Cormorant*, was docked. Brandon parked his bike and unlocked the security gate that led to the slip where his sailboat sat bobbing peacefully in the harbor. The cabin of the *Cormorant* was fitted with every amenity the young man needed for a week or two of sailing. He often took his boat out for long voyages whenever he could and never felt alone at sea. Instead, it was as though he and his vessel were skimming across the surface of Poseidon's eye.

Brandon walked the narrow gangplank that led to the boat's stern and stepped down into the vessel's cabin. He powered on the electricity and got his spare laptop out from the overhead stow. He threw the laptop on his bed and then took off his suit jacket and shoes. The itching from the hair growing on his groin had begun to subside. He pulled his boxers down and inspected the brand left by the Order's henchman. Soon his body hair would cover the insignia entirely and he could, once again, walk around the house shirtless without his mother or sisters asking him a bunch of questions. Brandon took a tube of burn cream from his suit pocket and gently applied a bit more to the affected region, then plopped down on his bed with Olivier's flash drive in hand.

The computer's desktop was up and ready to go. Brandon inserted the flash drive and waited. The command screen of the operating system appeared, which was unusual. The USB scanned through all of the drivers, searching for something. When the flash drive was done commandeering the operating system, the Order's insignia filled the computer's screen. It was the first time Brandon had seen it digitally rendered. It hovered against a black background and then dissolved into a world map dotted by nine points of interest. The dots were located in different locations around the earth: New Zealand, Namibia, Argentina, Mongolia, Finland, Switzerland, Canada, Iceland, and Hokkaido. A robotic voice proceeded to address Brandon personally. As it began to speak, a video played that corresponded to the context of the voice's monologue.

"Brandon Tsang, the Order will evacuate all of its members to private cities that have already been constructed in the locations on the map you have just seen. You and your immediate family members will be relocated to Alpha One located in present day Switzerland. Alpha One is the capital of the New World and has been retrofitted with the most state-of-the-art security systems and technologically advanced infrastructure the world has ever known. All of your assets now belong to the Order's shell company known as the 'Omnus Corporation'. You have twenty-four hours from 21:46 on June 14th to contact your sponsor, Gregory Olivier, who will facilitate your extradition. Leave all of your belongings behind. Take only what you can carry on your person. Failure to report to your sponsor by the aforementioned time will result in your disavowal from the brotherhood along with the inevitable deaths of you and your loved ones.

"The Omnus Corporation has, as of this moment, usurped all government forces, and in the following

weeks will incite a global crisis to begin the process we call 'the collection'. At the close of this message, your hard drive will self-destruct rendering the drives and all data therein unrecoverable. Commit these instructions to memory and carry them out with a sense of urgency. Your life and the lives of your family members depend upon it."

Brandon sat back in awe. The idea of a clandestine organization having the power to control all of the governments in the world was incomprehensible to him. It seemed a logistical impossibility. In addition, he had no idea how to convince his mother to leave her dream home. She had personally selected all the wallpaper, paint schemes, furniture, bedding, and lighting. It was her magnum opus. Brandon resolved to lie to her. It would be the only way to get her to leave, especially now that Charlie was dead and gone. The computerized voice had also said that the Omnus Corporation had seized his family's assets. Brandon tried to get online so that he could check his accounts but just as he was connecting to his Wi-Fi his laptop began to heat up.

He grabbed the computer by its screen and ran topside. He held the device over the stern of the ship as it fizzled. Smoldering blue sparks shot out from behind the monitor and Brandon let what remained of his laptop fall into the sea.

He rode back home thinking of what he would say to trick his family. He settled on telling his mother that he was going to be moving out and that he wanted her opinion on possible homes to purchase abroad. She would undoubtedly freak out, but at least she wouldn't suspect anything during what would have to be a long plane ride. Before he broke the news to them he would call Olivier. When Brandon got home he went straight up to his room and locked the door. He turned on the shower to make sure no one could hear the phone call he was about to make. He then pulled out the cheap flip phone he had been given and called Olivier. As the phone rang Brandon got anxious. He was taking a giant leap of faith without knowing the Order's true scope or purpose but, thanks to Charlie's ambitions, the Tsangs were well beyond the point of no return.

"Brandon, you are calling much sooner than I'd imagined. Have you made your decision?" Oliver asked confidently.

"It doesn't seem that we have much of a choice. You've seized all of our assets?"

"I assure you that it is strictly a precautionary measure carried out for your protection. I am afraid that the events that are unfolding as we speak will, unfortunately, require the immediate disruption of the current monetary system. Your family's estate, however, will be completely secure. Now have you made your decision?" Olivier's tone elevated in pitch. He sounded slightly irritated at having to explain the Order's reasoning.

"Of course. I want my family to be safe."

"That is not an answer!" Olivier screeched shrewdly over the phone. The Belgian's impatience caught Brandon off guard and forced the young man to reassess the delivery of his acceptance of the Order's terms.

"Yes. I agree to the will of the Order."

"Very well. That is a response more suitable for a prince of the legion. Don't allow anyone to leave your property for the next fourteen hours and disengage your security system. Is that understood?" Olivier commanded.

"Yes. I'm pretty sure we'll all be asleep. What did you mean by 'prince of the legion'?"

"As you know, there are nine megacities within the Omnus network that, together, comprise the new world. You are to be the face, the spirit, and the body that will be seen standing at the helm of the capital, Alpha One. You will help safeguard our glorious enterprise. That is your commission. It is a lofty role and is also the reason we had to put you through such a harrowing gauntlet. The Order has to be sure that we have the best, brightest, and most capable human beings on the planet at our disposal. Congratulations, Brandon Tsang. By this time tomorrow, you will witness what you and your father's sacrifices have provided you. Until next we meet, this is goodbye."

"Goodbye." Brandon hung up the phone. Everything was happening so fast. He had no idea if he was doing right by his family or placing their necks inside a guillotine. Only time would tell. Brandon left his room and went downstairs to disable the security system. When he had finished he joined his two sisters in their living room for a fun night of watching saucy Korean romcoms.

Brandon and his sisters fell asleep together on the large sectional sofa unaware of the team of men silently entering their property. After everyone in the house had been sedated the Tsang family was quietly taken out of their home and placed into a large moving truck. In the cover of the night, the stealthy intruders staged a home invasion to throw off police. The covert team then slipped into the truck and drove away leaving Vivian Tsang's dream home behind.

∞

Brandon woke up sometime later in the most comfortable bed he had ever slept on. He was extremely light-headed and when he opened his eyes the room was spinning. After his vision had settled he saw that he wasn't in his bedroom or even his house. Brandon put two and two together quickly. He was in Alpha One, somewhere between France and Switzerland. He couldn't remember where exactly. Brandon stumbled to the closest set of doors and opened them. They led out onto a beautiful semicircular balcony ringed with a marble balustrade. The large balcony was one of three on the same floor of the giant home that overlooked perfectly manicured gardens filled with Cypress, Palms, and Pine trees. The aromatic smell of flowers floating on wafts of clean air made love to Brandon's nose. The Order had done well. He gazed out onto a spectacular view of a city that shined with bright, colorful lights just like Hong Kong's Victoria Harbor. Silent fireworks lit up the sky above a large quiet lake where the lone masts of sloops and cutters gently rocked back and forth. Alpha One was truly an incredible sight. It was more beautiful than any city Brandon had ever seen.

The young man happily went back inside the villa and explored its interior. The Roman-inspired villa was rectilinear in shape with an atrium in the middle that housed a crystal blue pool shrouded in ferns and manicured shrubs. The villa was only two stories tall but the first floor had thirty-foot ceilings, the second floor more intimate fifteen. The walls were made of a mixture of off-white stone of differing textures and the floors in every room were made of marble tiles of varying hues. There was no direct lighting in the entire villa. All the lights had been recessed into soffits and niches. The fixtures that were out in the open were designed with translucent shades or panes of frosted glass that diffused the light they gave off. Modern and classical art hung on the walls in every room of the house. Brandon recognized one of the abstract paintings that hung in the grand foyer from one of his father's favorite auction catalogs that he always left in the bathroom of the old house. It was a Chagall and it had to have been worth tens of millions of Euros. He then stepped into the bucolic courtyard and almost fell to his knees when he saw the sculpture that was to adorn his garden. It was Polykleitos' *Doryphoros* – the real one from the British Museum. How could it be, Brandon thought? The sculpture was worth an inestimable sum and yet there it was. He ran to it and pressed himself against the cool white marble. While running his hands over the smooth contours of the perfectly contoured anatomical sculpture, Brandon noticed a simple folded note placed at its base. He bent down and picked it up. The note smelled of fragrant flowers. He opened it and read:

Youth is no longer a treasure of the past, but a perennial in a garden of earthly delights.

- *Olivier*

What an incredible gift. The estate was overwhelmingly perfect. He knew at once that this was *his* home. His smiles turned into laughter as he stripped naked and dove into the heated pool. His sloshing around must have wakened his sisters. He could hear them giggling and running about the villa just as he had done. Brandon lay on his back, floating in the middle of the pool while looking up at the sumptuous purple night sky. There was no light pollution and Brandon could see every star there was to see. He breathed in the pristine mountain air and smiled the grandest smile of his life. Every cell in his body felt free and uninhibited. There were no clouds on Brandon Tsang's horizon, only empty, virtuous skies. Killing his father had been the best thing Brandon had ever done. The old man was a malignant tumor that had been removed from Brandon's emotional body. Now he could truly live his life free from reproach or his family's indignation. As waves of unrelenting joy passed through Brandon's body he couldn't help but think of the Dutchman's soft orange beard and hazel eyes.

CHAPTER ELEVEN

Goodbye, Again

After Red Moses's men burned the village Tutu Town's chieftains sent Cecil, one of Darius's best martial arts students, north to take photographs of the building project Peter had told them about. A little more than a week later Cecil returned with a digital camera filled with images of a massive construction site. The elders called a town hall meeting where the photos were projected onto a wall for all to see. More than a thousand people showed up to discuss the implications the photos would have on their village.

Xavier was in charge of the projector and as he scrolled through the pictures he suddenly stopped. Not sure what he was looking at, the engineer zoomed in on a particular image to get a better look. Everyone in attendance gasped in horror. No one had any idea what or who the fearsome creatures in the photos were. A fervor began to foment until the building itself seemed to tremble. Leila and Angela, who were sitting in the back of the hall, looked at each other fearfully while the chieftains bickered with one another concerning the nature of the frightening beings. Leila could see Darius, seated next to the projector, staring at the images wide-eyed. She now understood the cryptic warning the Setian guard had given her while leaving the shelters. The Setians were using children as laborers *en masse*. They could be seen carrying out many different tasks in the photos being shown. Leila wondered if Megan and Marsaleh were somewhere in the work camps. An illogical desire to be reunited with her friends overtook her.

Darius had confessed to Leila that the village chieftains hadn't taken her advice. They had let Peter go but failed to chase down Red Moses. Now they were staring down the muzzle of an all-out war with beings whom they hadn't even imagined existed. Red Moses would most likely be back to terrorize Tutu Town again by taking even more people unless something was done about it. Angela, fed up with the ignorance of the chieftains, stood up and addressed the congress.

"You have made a mistake and your mistake will cost more lives. You should have listened to the girl, but instead, you let Red Moses go free. He will return and next time he will bring the Chitahuri with him!" The villagers shuddered at the thought of the mythical monsters they had all heard about as children growing up. Leila now knew people would listen to the truth concerning what she had been through.

"I know what they are!" Leila yelled after Angela had gotten the attention of everyone in the room. "I know what the lizard people are!"

Everybody in the hall turned toward the young girl. The chieftains signaled for Leila to say what was on her mind and so she began to tell her story - the complete version - including the part where the Setian guard warned her to stay away from the north. Her testimony surprised most of those who had gathered and sparked a great debate as to what the town should do in response to the looming threat.

Leila sat back down and was quite pleased with her delivery. By the look on everyone's faces she was sure that the villagers had believed every bit of her tale. Angela gave her a big hug and began to scold her for not telling her the truth earlier. The room was in a frenzy and none of the villagers could agree on what they should do next. Most of the young men in the village, including Darius, wanted to fortify the town and recruit young men from other townships to create a standing army. Others wanted to disband the village altogether and seek refuge elsewhere, possibly far to the south or northwest. And the last group, which included Xavier and a handful of other people, wanted to destroy the roads that led in and out of Tutu Town, especially the highway that crossed into Malawi. The chieftains decided to reconvene the next day so that they could confer with one another in private and then render their decision publicly.

Earlier, Xavier had picked Angela and Leila up for the town meeting. The small house on the hill had been miraculously spared. The marauders must have seen that there was nobody home when they had driven by it during their raid of the countryside. Xavier offered to return the ladies to the cottage and Angela happily accepted.

"Leila, why didn't you tell us about the Setians before?" Darius wanted to know. He shook his head as they drove down the long road to Angela's home.

"Because you wouldn't have believed me. You had to see it for yourselves. What are you going to do?"

"I don't think it is safe to live here any longer," Angela woefully admitted.

"Even if the chieftains decide to stay and fight I don't believe anyone will listen. The villagers are very afraid of these creatures and Red Moses," Xavier added.

"Yes, I think this is true," Angela agreed. "There are plenty of other places to live in Africa. The only problem is how to get there."

"How do we know there aren't more of those building sites in other places?" Darius questioned sensibly. "There could be tons of them all over the continent and we would never know."

"Leila, what do you think the town should do?" Xavier asked after realizing the little girl had provided accurate intel during both Peter's interrogation and in the town hall. He began to see her as a scout of sorts. It meant a lot to Leila that he would ask for her opinion.

"I want to see it: the Setian city. But I'm also scared. Maybe we should all go somewhere else. Somewhere where they have electricity like here," Leila answered.

"I feel the same way," Darius said, looking back at the young girl smiling. "You are a special little human being. You know that, don't you?"

It was always easy for Darius to make the young girl smile. When they arrived at Angela's cottage they got busy preparing a big feast to celebrate life and what would most likely be their last meal together. Angela said she would make a plate for the spirits so that they would help to guide their way forward. Angela revealed that her sister lived in a small coastal fishing village not so far from Tutu Town. She said that she would go there if the other villagers decided to leave. As much as Leila loved Angela, she didn't want to go live with another stranger in a stinky little fishing town. She wanted to go somewhere where the people weren't afraid to fight if the Setians ever showed up.

The small group of friends ate fresh papaya, yellow rice, and garlic potatoes together. They drank wine and the four of them danced to the rhythms of Angela's toy record player until nightfall. Xavier and Darius decided to sleep over, much to Leila's amusement. The group of friends eventually took their party outside and made a raging bonfire in the backyard. They took turns telling one another scary stories. Xavier told the scariest one. It was about an evil old sailor who trolled the wharfs at night looking for unlucky street urchins to nab so that he could sell them to witches who would pluck out their eyeballs and use them to see into the future. After storytelling time was over Xavier went to his truck and returned with an oversized bottle of warm champagne. He had been saving it for a special occasion. Xavier shared it with everyone including Leila. But, instead of the golden bubbles perking up the band of friends, their moods focused on the reality of their situation.

"I don't want to stay now that I think about it," Darius said, looking up at the stars. "There are still so many other places we could live."

"Yeah," Leila answered, smiling.

"Well, wherever we go we should go together," Xavier added, putting his arm around Darius's shoulder. "Between the both of us we can speak almost every major language in the world."

"I will go to my sister's village." Angela was serious. Her words had a tone of finality to them. She was the only one who knew exactly what she was going to do. "I will take Shema on my moto and we will go live by the sea. I've always wanted to live near the ocean. I love to eat fresh fish."

"I love you guys. I don't want us to split up." Leila said with tears in her eyes. She put her arms around Angela and didn't let go.

"You can come with us, Leila. We'll go to Israel. There are rumors that they're still using nuclear energy there," Xavier replied. "We'd love to have you. Who knows who we might have to interrogate along the way? Haha."

They all laughed knowing that their time together was at an end. They slept underneath the stars that night comforted by each other's company. The love they shared eclipsed the fear that many of the other villagers were experiencing that night. In a few hours, they would all have to make fateful decisions that would reverberate across the universe changing their lives for better or for worse.

∞

The next day at the town hall meeting there were far more people than had attended the previous day. As things got underway people had already started hugging each other and saying their farewells. Rumor was the chieftains couldn't come to a consensus on what needed to be done. And as the eldest chieftain, a kind man, took to the podium everyone quieted down to hear him speak.

"My brothers and my sisters, I -- like many of you -- was born in Tutu Town. It is a wonderful place to be from. I live in the same house that my grandfather built with his own hands. For a long time, we lived in peace even while many of our brothers and sisters from other places did not. Tutu Town is a village that welcomes strangers and foreigners alike. We have big hearts and big bellies. Indeed, the chieftains cannot agree on what to do. We do not have enough young men to fight. And I fear we do not have enough time to recruit more fighters from other villages. I have sent my favorite pigeon to a good friend of mine who lives on a big property in Botswana. We have a long-standing arrangement that will allow us to go and live on his lands. The man they call Red Moses will come back to harm us once again.

When he comes and finds that we have all gone he will look for other villages close by. Botswana is too far away for him to travel carrying such a large cargo. I believe it will be safer for us there. So, by order of the Council of Elders, I hereby declare Tutu Town to be evacuated. If you wish to stay here we will not be responsible for what happens to you. I am sorry that we cannot give you more protection, but this is our decision. If you do not know what to do please feel free to follow me and my family to Botswana. We will be leaving tomorrow morning. Thank you so much, but today is a day that we must all say goodbye to one another."

The elder stepped away from the lectern and solemnly shook hands with everyone around him. Leila was moved to tears to see so many friends and family parting ways. It was as clear as day that the chieftain's decision had pleased everyone. No one wanted to fight. Their fear of the Setians had won the day. Leila hugged Angela for the last time knowing what her plans were. She didn't let go until Darius approached them both.

"So, little one, will you come with us?" Darius asked. "Xavier and I have decided to make the trip to Israel. It's time we learned how to speak Hebrew."

"How long will it take you to get there?" Leila asked, looking up at Angela.

"You mean 'us'. It will take about a week if we drive non-stop," Darius answered. "We can practice Wing Chun along the way and camp underneath the stars every night. Sounds fun, right?"

"Yeah, it does. Okay, I'll go." Leila began to cry uncontrollably. She couldn't bear the thought of parting with Angela who had become an adoptive mother to her just like Marsala. Darius embraced the young girl and they all wept together. It was truly a sad day for everyone in Tutu Town.

"It'll be okay, Leila. You'll see," Darius promised.

"I'm gonna miss you so much," Leila admitted as she wiped the tears from her eyes. "Please come with us. Please! I promise I'll feed Shema every day."

"No, my love. I must look after my sister now. If things get worse she will need me by her side." Angela said smiling, "You must go and collect your things. I will stay here and help Dr. Mebina and her family pack up supplies from the hospital. They have decided to come with me to my sister's village. Leila, make sure you say goodbye to Shema before you go. She will miss you very much." They shared a moment looking into each other's eyes. "You are like a daughter to me, Leila. I always knew this day would come but it has come too soon. Please remember me when you look up at the moon and know that I, too, will be thinking of you. Now, go, and have as many new and wonderful adventures as you can."

"Okay," Leila sniffled. Sensing it was time to go, Leila drank in Angela's bright, sunny smile one last time. Afterward, she turned to Darius and left with him to find Xavier. The crazy-haired engineer was waiting for them outside in the Land Rover. Once Leila hopped in, Xavier drove to the apartment he and Darius shared.

The three friends began packing everything they would need for their epic journey. Leila's mood lightened as she found pleasure in watching her two friends argue over what was and wasn't necessary for their trip. Darius insisted that he needed his wooden dummy to practice his Kung Fu while Xavier did his best to explain how his geological soil sampling kit, as big as a grill, would be indispensable to them on the road. It took four hours to get all their gear either packed in the boot of the truck or strapped to the roof.

They then drove Leila to Angela's cottage. The young girl quickly and quietly packed the short list of items in her possession. She also nabbed a framed photo of Angela on her way out knowing her friend wouldn't mind. As Leila walked to the car she made sure to hug Shema and tossed the playful dog a few treats and then jumped back into the SUV. Leila buckled herself into the backseat and held up her tiny backpack. She laughed at the two men whose method of packing had neither been fast nor practical. Xavier pulled away from the house and began driving down the hill toward the main road. Leila turned around and waved goodbye to Shema, who ran after the car barking like she always did. Another chapter of Leila's life was closing. She was hopeful for what the future had in store and trusted Xavier and Darius implicitly. They were the best travel companions to have in a world filled with danger and uncertainty.

There was only one major freeway leading out of Mozambique. It went north and south cutting through the eastern half of Malawi. Xavier assured his friends that even though the highway was the same one Red Moses's men used to attack Tutu Town there was nothing for them to worry about. The plan was to drive north along the western edge of Lake Malawi until they came to the Trans-African freeway that stretched all the way to Cairo. After exploring the savannahs, hiking Kilimanjaro, and scaling the Egyptian pyramids, the trio would head toward Jerusalem. Everyone was excited about the journey and by the time they crossed into Malawi the fear of running into Red Moses lessened considerably.

Their first night on the road was spent camping alongside the very southern tip of the beautiful and grand Lake Malawi. It was an unbelievable experience for Leila who was extremely grateful for the chance to be around water once again. When morning came she begged Xavier to stay until midday so that she could swim in the sun. He agreed and received more kisses on his cheek in the span of a single minute than he had in his entire lifetime. Xavier warned the young girl of the dangers to be found in Africa's freshwater lakes: parasites, hippos, sea snakes, and more. Leila was undaunted and skipped to the water's edge, carrying Xavier's flippers and Darius's snorkel, without a care in the world.

The rippling waters of the picturesque lake sent the young girl's spirit soaring into the stratosphere. She counted the different species of colorful fish that swam beside her among the volcanic rocks that were spread out on the lakebed. The water was so clear that she could see all the flora and fauna in great detail. Leila felt like a dolphin as her thin body twisted and twirled through a liquid realm filled with mysterious animals and wondrous, wobbling light. It was the most fun Leila had enjoyed since the onset of the collection. After hours of uninterrupted swimming, Darius called Leila to shore for lunch. She didn't want to get out but had worked up a serious appetite. The three friends sat together on the grey-pebbled beach eating dried peppered beef sandwiches and salty potato chips. When they had finished eating and enjoying the cool breezes whizzing off the lake it was time to get moving again. Xavier had miscalculated the length of Lake Malawi and had reached its northern tip much sooner than expected. Much to Leila's disappointment, her first swim in the lake would be her last. That same night they camped on a hill overlooking the giant body of water. Leila couldn't understand why it was called a 'lake' and not a 'sea' even after Xavier did his best to explain the difference. Leila was sure that Lake Malawi was, in fact, a sea because it was so big.

The next morning they caught up with the Trans-African highway that led through Tanzania. They were making excellent time, that is until Darius saw a waterfall off to the east. Much like Leila begging to swim, Darius insisted Xavier stop the truck so that he could practice a yoga routine beside the falls. Darius said that 'he needed to calm the fiery spirits within him'. Xavier thought it hilarious but agreed. He and Leila made countless jokes as Darius bent himself into odd shapes, dramatically changing his poses as though he were being filmed on a movie set.

Tanzania was the most remarkable place Leila had ever seen. Gazelles, zebra, water buffalo, giraffes, lions, and elephants could all be seen from the relative safety of the Land Rover. Xavier had a nice camera with a powerful zoom and they all took turns photographing the romantic landscape from the relative safety of the highway.

Heavy rains came and went and the orange SUV kept great pace. Xavier and Darius had stockpiled plenty of water, ammunition, and fuel before leaving Tutu Town so their need to stop and trade was minimal. They drove on for a full day without seeing signs of labor camps or Setians anywhere. Just as they had begun to forget about why they were running in the first place, they came upon another highway that intersected with the one they were on. It was filled with travelers, many on foot, heading west.

"Hey, I'm pretty sure that highway goes straight through the northern Congo," Xavier informed his friends. He looked at the steady pace of the travelers in disbelief. Compared to the highway they were on it was jam-packed.

"What the hell is going on?" Darius questioned. He couldn't understand why so many people were headed in the same direction. "They can't be going to the labor camps? That wouldn't make any sense."

"Let's find out," Xavier said turning the truck around. He exited the turnpike leading to the traffic ridden freeway and parked the Land Rover in the shade of the overpass. Xavier got out of the truck and went out to investigate. Darius and Leila got out as well but only to stretch their legs. In a few minutes Xavier returned, shaking his head.

“Everyone says there are jobs in the west. They’re all going to the Congo.”

“Really?” Leila asked, bewildered. She had thought the Setians were in dire need of laborers and that’s why they had kidnapped the villagers from Tutu Town. She began to think that maybe there was another purpose behind the Setians’ intentions. There must have been if this many people were traveling such a long distance to find work and food. “Maybe the Setians don’t need workers. Maybe they just want to scare people out of their homes.”

“Well, if that’s the case then they succeeded,” Darius replied, wiping the sweat from his brow. “It’s bloody hot out here, isn’t it?”

“I wanted to see Mt. Kilimanjaro, but after seeing all these people I think I want to see what the lizards are building. I am sure we can get close enough without being swept up in the whole thing. And with this many people traveling there, it should be fine. What do you guys think?” Xavier asked.

“There’s a definite risk if we go. But, I must admit I’m rather curious myself,” Darius added. The two men looked at Leila as though she had the final say in the matter.

“I’m curious, too, but it’s dangerous. The Setian warned me not to go, remember?”

“Well, we don’t have enough fuel to make it to the Congo and then back north. We could probably find more fuel along the way, but...” Xavier looked at his friends who remained silent. “Okay, if we feel as though things are getting even slightly out of hand we’ll just double back. And if you guys change your mind on the way there, that’s cool too. Alright?” Xavier said, wanting everyone to feel good about their decision to venture off their intended course.

“Human beings…we’re just so damned curious, aren’t we?” Darius laughed while shaking his head. Xavier and Leila agreed and they all hopped back into the Land Rover and joined the traffic on the freeway toward their new destination. Leila was secretly joyful. She wondered if it was possible to see her friends from the shelters again, especially Marsala.

They made great time reaching the Congolese border by nightfall. The traffic had only swelled by road stands and rest stops. The rest of the freeway was more or less smooth sailing. Instead of camping for the night, everybody agreed to keep driving south so that they could hopefully reach the construction site before sunrise. They exited the highway and turned south traveling along the meandering Congo River. It was much different terrain than Tanzania and the roads were far more treacherous. Xavier blew a tire and the engineer took the opportunity to teach Leila how to replace it using the spare that was fastened to the back of the truck. It was challenging for Leila, especially because it was dark outside, but she got it done with Xavier's supervision. Since all the gear necessary for the job was out and ready to be used, Xavier decided to patch the old tire just in case they ran across any more problems. It took them an hour to complete both tasks before they were able to get back on the road.

Darius got behind the wheel so that Xavier could get some much needed sleep. The big man crawled into the back with Leila and within a few minutes they were both snoring away. Darius drove happily until the morning light. He sang the tunes of his favorite love songs to keep himself company. As the sun peeked over the mountains to the east, Darius found a nice quiet place to park on the top of a grassy plateau. The plateau overlooked a wide basin covered in lush tropical vegetation. The air was clean and crisp. Forest song from the valley below ascended into the morning sky like a sacramental offering. While his two friends slept, Darius greeted the day using the language of Ashtanga yoga. He breathed in and out as silently as a cumulus cloud gliding across the heavens. He finished his sacred routine by adopting the lotus position and watched the Setian city quietly become illuminated by the rising sun. Darius stared at the sprawling construction site without emotion. He was just close enough to view it with the naked eye. He could make out the city's massive walls and the jagged spires that rose up like crooked fingers from behind them. After a while Darius returned to the truck to rouse Xavier and Leila.

"Hey, would you like to see the city, mate?" Darius asked, rocking his big friend back and forth. "Where are your binoculars?"

Xavier didn't respond but Leila pushed herself up, wiping the sleep from her eyes. She knew where Xavier kept his binoculars and, after grabbing them, they went outside together to stand in awe of the enormous city.

"It's so big," Leila observed through bleary eyes. "We gotta get closer."

"I'm not sure if it's safe. Something tells me this is as close as we should get." Darius advised.

"Yeah, but Xavier's gonna wanna get closer so he can see what types of machines they're using to build it."

"Hmm," Darius sighed, "can I see the binoculars for a sec?"

The walls of the city were lustrous even though they appeared to be made of stone. All around the base of the walls were thousands of thatched roof dwellings. Just like in the photos, Darius could see hundreds of children already at work pushing wheelbarrows and carrying loads of building materials.

"That wall must be a hundred feet tall," Leila guessed, taking back the binoculars.

"I'd say more like sixty or seventy feet, luv. Look at all those people living outside it. You say those children are all from the collection?"

"I don't know. Maybe some of them," Leila replied. She sighed heavily at the thought of the toil Marsaleh might be experiencing at that very moment.

"Let's try and wake the big man again."

"Alright," Leila answered, running to the back doors of the Land Rover. She jumped on top of Xavier's belly. He still didn't budge. He was out like a light. "What do we do?"

"I guess it wouldn't hurt to drive a little closer. If we see trouble we'll just drive off," Darius suggested.

"Yeah, but we've gotta be careful," Leila reminded Darius. "We don't want to be seen."

Darius started the truck and drove back down the muddy road that lead away from the plateau and turned south. The road they were on had been carved out of the steep mountainside and there was a sharp drop-off on the left. As Leila looked out her window she could feel the goosebumps rising on her arms. Darius engaged the four-wheel drive to give the tires some extra traction. They got as close as Darius wanted to be and then headed east ascending a narrow set of winding switchbacks that snaked their way up to the very top of the mountain. By the time they got there, it was well into the morning. The blue shadows of dawn turned peach and gray-green as the light from the sun became stronger. Darius parked the SUV away from the edge of the mountaintop so that it couldn't be seen from below. He and Leila got out to investigate the building site but quickly realized they had made a mistake. They were way too close. From their vantage point, they were able to look down onto the entire operation. It was a colossal building project, the size of the entire city of New York, which Leila had seen, in person, twice.

"Get down, Leila," Darius ordered as he tugged at the young girl's sweatshirt. "If we can see them then that means they can sure as hell see us. Go wake that grumpy bastard up."

Leila took the mission seriously and slid backward away from her position on all fours so as not to be seen. She opened the truck's back door and began tickling Xavier's feet. She gave his foot a frightful tug. Xavier shot up and swiped at the air angrily. His face was as red as a beet and he eyed Leila with a crazed semi-conscious look. It took Xavier a few moments to calm down. When he was awake and after he drank a bottle of water they all laughed off Leila's rude awakening.

"Well done, Leila," Xavier snorted. "But all you had to do was ask me to get up."

Leila scoffed at the suggestion implying that the man was capable of sleeping through anything and sarcastically handed Xavier the binoculars.

"Take a look, Xavier. What do you see?" she said.

Xavier took the binoculars and crept to the mountain's ledge joining Darius. When Xavier saw the city his mouth dropped.

"First of all, this is way too close, you guys." Xavier put the binoculars to his eyes and began searching for details of the construction site. He kept quiet for a long time without speaking. "This site is incredible. They're running CAT-9 and fiber optic cable down there so we know they have access to satellites. They're using at least five tower cranes to build that wall which is well over sixty feet tall. The stones they're using are made to interlock with each other and appear to have been cut with great precision. Geez, there must be half a million workers down there! Look at all those poor kids. Ah, no wonder they need so many workers. I don't see a single power source anywhere. There must be one somewhere. Wow." Xavier could see a lot of advanced engineering principles being employed in the city's construction. The spires that rose above the walls looked as though they had been cast in one piece and erected as whole units. Complex scaffolding surrounding the tall structures and the laborers using them were attaching strange shielding to the spires' facades. Xavier whipped out a smaller digital camera from his vest pocket and began snapping away. He took dozens of photos of everything in sight and then stashed the camera away. "I don't see any lizard people or anyone being held without their consent. It looks like a normal work camp from up here."

"Yeah, it's true. I didn't see any lizards either," Darius added, as he backed away from the ledge on his elbows and knees. Xavier and Leila followed suit before standing up and walking back to the car.

"I'm sure the Setians are there. They're probably just inside the city," Leila reasoned. They got back into the Land Rover satisfied with what they had seen.

"Well, was it worth it?" Darius asked with a big grin on his face. "It cost us a day and a half and almost a full tank of gas."

“I say, yes. It was. How ‘bout you Xavier?” Leila wanted to know.

“That all depends.”

“Oh yeah, on what?” Darius teased.

“On whether those men coming up the road will let us leave alive,” Xavier answered, gripping the steering wheel tightly.

Leila whipped her head around toward the front of the truck. A dozen armed men were walking toward their SUV. One of them in particular wore black sunglasses, a red beret, and a red bandana around his neck. Leila couldn’t believe it. It was Red Moses. Even though she had never seen the man in person she remembered what he looked like from probing Peter’s past. She was sure it was him. The men were accompanied by three trucks that were blocking the entrance to the road. Leila screamed for Xavier to get the heck out of there.

“Gun it, mate!” Darius yelled. Xavier accelerated but hesitated. He couldn’t immediately justify running over Red Moses who was walking directly toward them blocking their escape. The African swung his rifle off of his shoulder and pointed it at the Land Rover. He began to shout orders at Xavier who couldn’t understand anything the man was saying.

"Xavier, drive! Go!" Leila pleaded.

"Put your seatbelts on!" Xavier ordered as he slammed down the gas pedal. He surged forward directly at Red Moses who fired off a single round directly into the truck's radiator but had to jump to the side to avoid the accelerating truck. Xavier plowed through the blockade of vehicles that had been parked at the crest of the hill. On his way through, the SUV took on a barrage of gunfire. Several bullets sped through the windshield and cracked it like a spider web. The cracks made it incredibly hard to see through the glass. Still, Xavier drove on recklessly down the treacherous mountain road.

"Kick it out the windshield, Darius. Hurry! Kick the damn thing out." Xavier ordered.

Darius used both of his legs to smash through the windshield. After his third thrust, the entire pane flew forward. The dented trucks that had been part of the blockade had begun to give chase. They were shooting at the Land Rover from behind. Xavier accelerated trying his best to put as much distance between them and their pursuers as possible. Leila screeched in fear as bullets whizzed into the truck's cabin. She had never been shot at and didn't know what to do.

“Leila, get down. Keep your head down!” Darius shouted at the young girl from the front seat. He then looked at Xavier. “Where’s your bloody gun?”

“In the glove box. The safety’s on, but it’s loaded,” Xavier answered as he continued to charge down the winding mountain pass. Darius frantically searched for the gun. After finding it he climbed into the back seat and cranked open the manual lever that controlled the sunroof. He weaseled his way through all the gear strapped to the roof of the SUV and started taking potshots at the trucks who were steadily gaining on them. One of his shots hit the driver of the lead truck in the throat. Darius cursed in delight as he watched the vehicle careening off the road and crash into the ravine below. There were two more trucks in pursuit. “C’mon, go faster! Drive! That’s it.” Darius yelled at Xavier as he pounded the side of the roof by the driver’s side.

Darius took a calculated risk. He began to undo the straps that held all of their gear to the Land Rover’s roof rack. Once Darius untied the last strap the container filled with their spare fuel tumbled behind the SUV along with their grill and the portable generator. Darius aimed the handgun at the tumbling container of gasoline and emptied the clip. Luckily, one of the bullets found its mark. A powerful explosion blasted the side of the mountain, engulfing the next truck in a furious blaze of burning petrol. The truck's occupants jumped out of the moving inferno covered in accelerant and flames. Several of them were run over by the last truck as they rolled on the ground in a desperate attempt to put out the fires that engulfed them mercilessly.

"What the hell, Darius?" Xavier shrieked as the truck caught the percussion wave of the explosion and fishtailed dangerously over the edge of the road. Xavier gripped the wheel expertly and brought the rear tires back on course. The engineer was upset that Darius had let loose their most treasured belongings. "Dammit, Darius! Get back inside. Leila! Pull him in!"

Leila did as she was asked. She yanked on Darius's yoga pants but they just slid down to reveal his boxer shorts. Darius got the hint and ducked back down into the cabin after hoisting up his pants.

"Darius! Why the hell would you throw out our fuel?"

"What the hell was I supposed to do?" Darius countered, frustrated at his friend's lack of appreciation. "I've offed two of them. Just keep driving."

Darius was about to climb back into the passenger seat when he noticed a man in the truck following them lean out of his passenger side window. He pulled out a rocket propelled grenade launcher but was having a hell of a time lining up his target on the bumpy mountain pass.

"Oh shit. Oh shit! They've got RPGs!" Darius shouted. He jumped over Leila who was cowering in the backseat and desperately searched around the boot of the truck for the tire iron. He eventually found it and began smashing the rear window open. Darius finally busted through the glass and watched as the rear windshield twirled away behind the SUV. He then grabbed the patched tire from the back and threw it at the truck seconds before the man fired off his RPG. The driver swerved to avoid the truck tire which caused the missile to sail slightly off course. The rocket miraculously flew straight through the cab of the Land Rover eventually exploding into the face of the mountain some two hundred meters in front of them. The blast dislodged huge chunks of rock which began to fall and block sections of the narrow pass. Thankfully, Xavier made it through right before a shower of boulders fell onto the road. The enormous rocks blocked the advance of the last truck. Unfortunately, just as the Land Rover sped away from their attackers, a massive rockslide began.

"Holy crap. Xavier, we've got to get off the road, now!" Darius shouted as he witnessed the deadly avalanche crush the men in the last truck like an empty beer can. In seconds, their pursuers were buried in tens of meters of loose dirt. The rock slide continued down the mountainside building momentum and mass as it went. Xavier understood that there was no way to outrun the falling rock by using the switchbacks which would only bring them back into the avalanche's trajectory time and again. The engineer gunned it, hoping to make it to the next bend in the road before they were pummeled to death.

"Everybody make sure you're strapped in! This is going to get nasty," Xavier yelled over his shoulder. Darius and Leila made sure their restraints were on as tight as possible. Xavier was only a hundred meters away from reaching safety when a lone boulder, hurtling itself ahead of the rockslide like a rogue meteor, shot through the cab of the Land Rover. The rock bashed Xavier's head with the force of a cannonball and then exited the driver's side window. The blow had broken the engineer's skull, killing him instantly. His prone body leaned forward against the wheel causing the SUV to veer wildly off the road. Leila screamed in horror as Darius shielded her eyes from the awful scene. The tragic moment enveloped Darius, who saw things unraveling around him in slow motion. Certain of his own death, Darius knew what he had to do: protect Leila. Darius unstrapped himself, wrapped his body around the young girl, and held onto her as tightly as possible without hurting her. The Land Rover, dead man at the wheel, launched itself off of a small berm and flew through the air. The SUV hit its rear fender on a tree which spun it around like a top. After tumbling over and over the mangled truck finally came to a rest between two large rocks that stood proudly out of the mouth of the mighty Congo River.

∞

The tug of fast moving water pulled Leila out of her unconsciousness. As she opened her eyes the pain from a cut on her head flared to the fore. Her body was dangling halfway inside the powerful current of the river. Someone had propped her up on a ledge just above the water. It had to have been Darius. Her body hurt all over and she was completely disoriented. The world was spinning and the young girl threw up all over herself. Leila managed to sit up while trying hard to get a better grip on the situation. Her vision was blurred but she was still able to see the crumpled Land Rover upside down upriver. Its bright orange frame had been beaten to hell and all of their belongings were being carried downstream. She could see Xavier's body hanging halfway out of his seat belt. His arm was stretched out of the sunroof, his bloody fingers just inches away from the water's surface. Leila cried out for Darius who she couldn't see anywhere. Her head throbbed horribly every time she screamed. That's when she saw movement on the banks by the overturned

SUV. It was Red Moses and his men. She could see his red bandana from where she sat. It was like a beacon of death. He pointed at the little girl from beyond the wreckage of the truck and several men began to ford the river toward the opposite bank.

Leila cried out for Darius again, but there was no answer. She had to do something. She refused to be taken by the men and sold into the Setian labor camps or worse. The young girl looked around one last time, trying to find her beloved friend but there was no sign of him anywhere. Leila took a deep breath and then plunged into the river. The turbulent waters carried her a great distance from Red Moses's men rather quickly. Leila did her best to be brave as the torrent pushed her body along its winding course like a bird caught in a violent storm. She spilled over a small two-meter fall and hit her cast on a rock underneath the water. A jolt of intense pain shot through her leg as her ankle jammed upward against her tibia. Leila screeched, taking in a mouthful of water. It felt as though she had broken her ankle again. After the falls the river gained momentum dramatically even though its surface became calmer. Some great force ahead was pulling Leila toward it. She tried to look for anything she could grab onto. The only thing she could see were the roots of the mandrakes on the banks, but they were too far away for her to reach. She had to get closer to the banks if she wanted to escape the river. Leila began to hear a deep rumbling noise filling the air around her. She could hear it even more while underwater. She lifted her chin to see what it was. When she finally got a glimpse of what lay just one hundred meters away she began to panic. It was a gigantic waterfall. There was no way to tell how far the drop was but Leila knew instinctively that she would not survive it. Images of Darius's dead body spilling over the falls flashed through the young girl's mind. She had to get to the banks of the river. She had to survive. Otherwise, Darius and Xavier's sacrifice would be for nothing.

Thankfully, Leila's cast got stuck between two rocks in the middle of the river. She dunked her head to investigate and curiously spied a handful of speckled fish swimming lazily behind the rocks on the river bottom. They were letting the rocks break the current for them. She went back up to take a breath then submerged her head again to take a better look. The fish gave her an idea. Leila would let the rocks do the work. She looked downstream for the next big rock. After freeing her foot, she pushed off toward it and eventually slammed against it. Even though the current was unrelenting, she found hope in the fact that her idea was working. Leila went below again looking for her next target. It was much further away but was just as large. There would be no room for error in her approach. If she missed the next rock she would be swept over the falls, whose roar was now so loud it drowned out everything else. The young girl crept toward the rock's right edge and instead of pushing off, she let the flow simply take her. She found the rock with no problem and held onto it for dear life. There were no more stones big enough to help her reach the river's edge. Her only chance to save herself was a lone craggy root that stuck out over the muddy banks like the arm of an angel. Leila had to make it. Her heart raced as she leaped toward the direction of the mandrake root. She stretched her body as taut as she could and reached for the root. Her heart lifted as her wet fingers grabbed onto her only lifeline as tight as a vice. She began to pull her battered body closer to the banks. The mandrake root started to give way under her weight. Leila frantically clawed her way up the riverbank making it to safety just as the old dried out root snapped. She watched the branch get carried away and disappear over the falls in between harried breaths for air. Her energy spent, Leila fell on her back and looked at the sun breaking through the forest canopy. She was hurt, frightened, and exhausted. The din of the falls lorded over her awareness causing her to temporarily forget that Red Moses' men were still after her. Through the fugue of agony, she could hear men off in the distance bickering with each other. There was no telling how far away they were but it was enough motivation for the little girl to gather herself and continue limping toward her freedom.

Leila walked downstream. She wanted to see the waterfall that almost claimed her life. There was no footpath so she had to carefully step between moss-covered stones and loose treefall without slipping. She finally got a good look at the majestic waterfall. It was as deadly as it was gorgeous. The roiling river careened over the falls a full hundred meters, splashed into its plunge pool, and then continued at a more leisurely pace. Leila noticed a gap in between the curtain of falling water and the cliff face it roared over. It was dangerous but she saw that it might be possible for her to climb onto the shallow footholds jutting out of the hard rock which led into the cavity behind the cataract. It looked like an excellent place to hide. Leila thought about it for a moment and decided to go for it. Red Moses's men wouldn't suspect a young girl to be brave enough to try the deadly climb. She would have to be careful as her cast would complicate her negotiation of the cliff face. Leila wasted no time.

It took a while but Leila eventually made it across the span of miserly footholds. She ended up on a thick, wide stone ledge whose outer edges had been smoothed to match the contours of the waterfall perfectly. Leila felt at home, safe behind the falls. She curled up behind one of the boulders and let the soothing cadence of the falls lull her to sleep.

The pain in her ankle woke Leila up. She slowly stood and could tell by the amount of pressure she put on it that she hadn't broken it again. The young girl sat on top of one of many large flat boulders and watched the waterfall curve overhead. She couldn't understand why the universe had taken Xavier and Darius away from her. It seemed that every time she got close to someone they were ripped from her life. Even Ruby, her pet snake, had been taken from her by mandrills. There was no one to explain what was happening to her so she began to blame herself.

Red Moses's men hadn't found her yet. She began to hope that maybe they thought that she had also fallen victim to the mighty falls. Leila quietly sobbed to herself as she thought about her friends. Why had they been so stupid as to leave the solace of the savannahs? They were free, but, no, they had to see the Setian city for themselves even after being warned not to go. Now, Leila was all alone again and soon she would need to find something to eat. Part of her simply wanted to get up, walk through the thundering curtain of water and surrender herself.

Leila had no idea what to do. It was still too soon to venture out from behind the protection of the falls so she began to stack rocks in memory of her friends. Leila had learned how to stack rocks while on a school field trip. She had always wanted to try it again, but, until now, never had a reason. While searching for a flat stone she spied a cave at the back of the ledge large enough for a person to walk inside it. She wondered where it led to and ventured toward it, keeping an eye out for stones she could use. When Leila got close to the cave's entrance she heard heavy breathing coming from inside. The tiny hairs all over her body stood on end, causing the young girl to freeze in her tracks. Something really big was inside.

"Who's in there?" Leila yelled. "I know you can see me!"

There was no answer but Leila could hear that the breathing was labored. Whoever or whatever was inside the cave was probably wounded or sick. Leila took another step toward the opening but was halted by the most threatening roar a human child could ever hear. Leila screamed out in fear and ran behind a nearby boulder. She cautiously peeked her head around the rock to see if the monster had come out.

"That was mean!" She shouted. "You didn't have to do that. I'm no threat to you. I'm only ten!"

Leila, bitten by a mixture of brazen curiosity and the fear of being alone, approached the cave opening again. This time she was ready for any more sudden outbursts. Whatever was inside remained silent and as Leila crept closer and closer she was able to make out a pair of narrow yellow eyes gleaming at her.

"I knew you were a Setian," she said confidently, squatting just inside the cave. "Don't worry, you're not the first one I've met. I know you're hurt. I can tell by how you breathe. Can I help you?"

The Setian didn't answer. He just sat there wheezing, his eyes never leaving the young girl. So, Leila did what any little girl afraid to be alone did, she talked. She sat there and told the Setian her entire life story right down to the final moment when she lost Darius and Xavier. She didn't cry this time. Instead, she kept looking for rocks to build her memorial.

"Hey, are there any flat stones over there by you? I need some flat ones to build grave markers for my friends," Leila said matter-of-factly. The creature didn't answer. Several moments later two flat stones flew in Leila's direction. They landed right in front of her feet and, seeing that they were perfect, she thanked the creature for his help.

Leila decided to leave the Setian alone for a while and went back to creating her memorial. She was doing quite well stacking six differently-shaped stones on top of one another. Six stones for the six people she had lost: her mother and father, Jacob, Xavier, Darius, and a little stone to represent all the other people she had lost. Leila was proud of her sculpture and, with a sharp-edged stone, began to carve the names of her loved ones on the ground in front of the rock stack. It took her over an hour to scratch their names into the hard bedrock and when she was done she stood back and admired her work. She thought that her friends would be pleased with the care and effort she took to create such a monument to their honor. She began to think about the Setian again. She knew he was suffering, probably even close to death. With the best intentions, Leila walked back to the cave and squatted down at its mouth. She didn't speak right away but searched the darkness for the golden eyes. She found them blinking with almost every painful breath.

"If you tell me your name I will carve it next to my friends' names," she said mournfully and with a great deal of sincerity. Another long silence followed.

The creature eventually spoke to Leila in a tone that was rushed due to exertion, not rudeness, "Buce…pha…los. Bucephalos," the Setian strained.

Leila could see that it had taken a great deal of effort for him to speak.

"Thanks," she said. "I won't ask you any more questions, Bucephalos. I know it's hard for you to talk. I'll go write your name. I don't think I will spell it right, but I promise I'll make it look nice."

Leila went back to her death memorial and began carving Bucephalos's name above Darius' to keep them in alphabetical order. As she worked an intense spirit of compassion overtook her. Her heart was filled with sadness, not for herself, or even for her friends, but for the creature who was in the cave dying by himself, quietly. She was reminded of Ruby's red body pierced in the side by the talons of the nasty sea hawk. The little girl continued to carve the creature's strange name into the stone ledge until her fingers bled. After she had finished, she dropped her tools and returned to the cave opening. It was getting dark outside and the sun's bright orange light had been replaced by thin gray shadows lit by a waxing moon. Leila decided she would try to approach the beast to carry out what she deeply felt was her responsibility. She wouldn't let the Setian die alone.

"I'm going to sit with you, Bucephalos. I'm not scared of you and I won't try to hurt you. I just don't want you to have to be alone," Leila promised. She searched again for the Setian's golden eyes but they were closed. Leila crawled toward the creature and witnessed the true extent of the Setian's injuries. His left leg was badly mangled and his muscular torso bore deep gashes that were still bleeding. Bucephalos had been seriously injured by someone or something. Leila leaned next to him and put her head against the right side of his abdomen. To her surprise, Bucephalos lifted his right arm and laid it across the girl's body. And at that very moment, the same spiritual energy that Leila had felt while carving the Setian's name in the stone returned once again but with much more intensity. A bright shining light appeared from out of nowhere within the cave followed by a series of high-pitched tones that enveloped the girl and the Setian's senses. Bucephalos opened his eyes and confronted the brilliance with his last living breath. Leila held onto the creature as though they were both about to be sucked into the frigid void of outer space. It was then that the same voice from Leila's dream spoke to her once again. The little girl welcomed the presence of the soft voice and instantly felt at peace with her desperate situation.

"Leila, my child. You are the brightest star in the sky. Your love has transcended your greatest fear. You cannot understand me now, but know this, the friendship born in this cave has forever changed the destiny of the Earth. Let darkness flee whenever the two of you are together. Blessed child, no longer will you be alone. Now rise and nurse your new friend back to health. Go and never forget this night."

ZZRRRRAAAAP!!! The dazzling light pierced every corner of the cave and tremendous flashes of heat rippled throughout its interior. Then, in a blink of an eye, the light shrunk into a glowing orb the size of a pea. The orb shone brightly against the blackness of the cave and lit up Leila's face and then sank into the young girl's forehead just above the bridge of her nose. The cave became dark again as everything around them returned to normal. Leila lifted her head and backed away from the Setian whose eyes were still as wide as saucers. It wasn't until Leila reached the entrance to the cave that the creature spoke to her.

"What have you done to me?" Bucephalos asked, his voice wavering. "How can this be?"

"I don't know. How can what be?" Leila's eyes were still filled with tears but they were tears of joy, not sorrow. The pain in her foot was gone. She flexed her ankle inside her cast without the slightest discomfort.

"What power is this?" the Setian asked almost in a whisper. "I can feel it in my entire body. I have been restored." He looked again at the little girl. His eyes blazing with conviction. "Who are you? Are you a human being?"

“My name is Leila,” she said chuckling a bit. She wiped her eyes with the back of her arm. “Yes, I’m human.”

“Grubs,” he said smiling. The Setian’s voice still sounded a little weak and strained.

“Grubs?” she asked almost laughing. “What do you mean? What is ‘grubs’?”

“I’m very weak. I must eat. You said that you wanted to help me?” he informed her. “Grubs...inside the caves… deep in the walls. You must stick your arm in the gaps and feel around for them.”

“Uh, okay. How many do you need?” she asked with a bit of trepidation.

“One. Just need one.”

“Okay. I’ll go,” Leila said, walking into the darkness of the cave’s interior. She followed Bucephalos’ instructions and when she could no longer see the light coming from the moon she started to feel around the walls for gaps in the rock. After trying several different holes, she finally felt something scurry past her fingertips. Leila reached her arm forward until her cheek pressed against the cool rock wall. She grasped at whatever was inside. Suddenly, something slimy latched onto her wrist. It must have been a grub. She pulled her hand out of the hole and ran toward the mouth of the cave where Bucephalos was waiting. When Leila stepped into the dim light she shrieked in horror. A giant bulbous worm-like monster was trying to eat her arm.

"Aagh! Get it off! Take it off. Hurry!" She shouted at Bucephalos who laughed so heartily that it was a sure sign that he had been healed.

"Well done! That's a big one," he chuckled. He took one of his claws and pinched underneath a portion of the grub's plating, just behind its head. The disgusting animal stopped moving immediately. The Setian then slid the slimy invertebrate off of Leila's arm and began tearing it apart like a human would a lobster.

Leila's arm was covered in an ooze that began to burn. She ran toward the waterfall to rinse the goo off but Bucephalos stopped her.

"I wouldn't do that. Water makes it worse," Bucephalos warned while gorging on a mouthful of grub.

"How do I stop the burning? C'mon, this isn't funny," Leila argued.

"There are only two ways for a human to stop the burning. One is to soak your arm in goat's milk, for a day. The other is to urinate on it. I don't see any goats. Haha."

"What?" Leila couldn't believe what she was hearing. She glared at the Setian who couldn't help but smile at her plight. "You'd better be telling the truth."

Leila went off on her own and urinated on her arm like the Setian told her to do. The burning went away instantly. She began to laugh. It was a cruel joke, but now that it was over she could see that it was also really funny. She rejoined Bucephalos who offered her some of the grub. She thumbed her nose at it and allowed him to finish eating it joyfully.

"Thank you," he said. "That was nourishing. But I require your help further. I must pack my wounds with the mud from the river. The worms inside it will clean them for me. Do you think you can do that?"

"As long as I won't have to pee on myself again, sure."

"No. Haha."

"I didn't know Setians had senses of humor."

"We don't. That is why I ended up dying alone in a cave."

The two of them shared a moment of brevity. Leila thought Bucephalos was funny. It felt so strange laughing with a Setian. They were so "evil-looking" that Leila never imagined one of them enjoying a good practical joke. In the spirit of jest, Leila walked over to the Setian and stuck her foot in his face while he was finishing up the last bites of his meal.

"Can you open my cast for me, please?" She giggled. Bucephalos slapped her cast so hard that Leila twirled around several times. The cast broke apart in mid-air and flew into the falls.

"Cool! That was so awesome!" Leila exclaimed. "How did you do that?"

Bucephalos just waved her off gesturing for her to get the mud for his wounds. Cloaked in nightfall the young girl left the comfort of the falls to go and collect the river mud for her new friend. She took great care to be as sneaky as possible. Red Moses' men could've been anywhere watching and waiting. Leila broke off several big green leaves growing alongside the riverbank and filled them with mud before rolling them up tightly. She made a half dozen more then hauled the mud back to the waterfall in her shirt which she had taken off and used as a pack. The chore was a challenging one but was made easier by the fact that Leila's hurt foot had been completely healed. Leila made it back to the falls with the mud. Bucephalos was still sitting in the same place waiting.

“Is this enough?” she asked, handing him seven rolled-up leaves filled with rich, dark brown mud.

“Yes, this is sufficient for now. I will need more in a few days.” Bucephalos took handfuls of mud and clumsily pushed them into the wounds that covered most of the left side of his body. His left thigh had received most of the damage and required the most mud. He handed Leila one of the empty leaves and asked her to collect a bit of water from the falls for him. She gladly hopped to it. It took her a couple of minutes to figure out how to contort the leaf so that it wouldn’t leak. She then walked the leaf back over to the Setian but didn’t hand it to him for fear the water would spill.

“You want me to pour it over the mud, right?” she asked.

“Yes, but not too much.”

She added just the right amount of water to the mud until it was the consistency of wet clay. The Setian tried to massage the mud into his wounds but his hands were simply too big for the job. Leila batted his claws away and used her nimble little fingers to press the mud deeply into his cuts. She was careful to spread it evenly keeping it flush with his scales.

“What happened to you? I mean, these look like bite marks!” Leila said, pointing to the reptilian’s left thigh.

“Dyklotimus happened to me,” Bucephalos answered gingerly poking the wounds on his face.

“What is Dyklotimus?”

“Who is Dyklotimus? He is a Setian of great power who took it upon himself to personally see to it that I died alone and in exile.”

“Why?”

“A group of workers mishandled an important piece of construction equipment. Dyklotimus ordered me to kill the men right then and there. I refused. In response, Dyklotimus then commanded the very same workers to kill me. When that proved difficult, he bit my leg and had me banished from my home. Dyklotimus is an Ok, and a bite from an Ok is toxic. That is why it was so hard for me to breathe when you first tried asking for my name. I should be dead by now. It was only the strength of your magic that kept me alive.”

“It wasn’t me. It was the voice. You heard it, didn’t you?

“I saw only a great light.”

“Oh…what is an Ok?”

“They are the Setian ruling class. They are much, much bigger than me and have tails.”

"I've seen one, in the shelters. He wore a black cloak. He was really scary."

"Yes, that was an Ok. They are as clever as they are cruel."

Leila continued to pepper the Setian with question after question. The two of them sat together for hours getting to know one another. Bucephalos had a quick wit and a nasty mouth which Leila found quite charming. The young girl spent the next couple of weeks nursing the reptilian back to health. She cleaned his wounds every few days by packing fresh mud onto them and even managed to capture more grubs for him. When Bucephalos had fully healed he taught Leila many things about Setians and their new capital city, Avandar, which was well on its way to being completed. Most importantly, he showed her how to negotiate her way underground without the use of a light source. Leila begged Bucephalos to take her to see Avandar up close but he always resisted. He didn't know how to explain to her that he was now 'drah gohn' which meant that he was forbidden to return to his city. There was little that could be done to appeal for clemency. Leila had healed the Setian's body but she didn't have the means to restore his relationship with his queen, who didn't take acts of insubordination lightly.

The Setians had abandoned their subterranean dwellings in favor of life on the surface. Leila and Bucephalos were able to move freely throughout the underground caverns without fear of confrontation. They became inseparable and often slept on top of one another like puppies behind the curtain of the waterfall where they first met. Their simple, yet natural desire to be kind to one another had unwittingly sparked a chain of events that would one day sweep over the human and Setian worlds alike. And while the Order played its devilish hand against the bulk of humanity, the fragile hope for a peaceful future grew quietly within the hearts of two unlikely friends living deep within the womb of Mother Earth.

MDW LTD Publishing is dedicated to distributing print, digital and musical works which truly fascinate and inspire fans to think differently and freely.

We are motivated by our authors, artists and creators as we strive to 'FEEDBACK,' to Forever Empower and Educate the Development of Breakthrough Artists and Creators of all Kinds.

We only work with creators we proudly believe in 100%. We find that this ensures our most authentic passionate work as creators. Due to the nature of this principle, and our in house marketing and promotional network, we thoroughly vet the work of our creators to maintain business of repute.

www.ingramcontent.com/pod-product-compliance
Lightning Source LLC
Chambersburg PA
CBHW060756310726
48980CB00002B/111

* 9 7 9 8 9 9 0 1 9 4 7 2 4 *